LIST

T0162502

ALSO BY DAVE GODFREY

The New Ancestors (1970)
Dark Must Yield (1978)

DEATH GOES BETTER WITH COCA-COLA

DAVE GODFREY

A
LIST

First published in 1967 by House of Anansi
This edition published in Canada in 2016 and the USA in 2016 by House of Anansi Press Inc.
www.houseofanansi.com

House of Anansi Press is committed to protecting our natural environment.
As part of our efforts, the interior of this book is printed on paper that contains
100% post-consumer recycled fibres, is acid-free, and is processed chlorine-free.

20 19 18 17 16   1 2 3 4 5

Library and Archives Canada Cataloguing in Publication

Godfrey, Dave, 1938–2015, author
Death goes better with Coca-Cola / David Godfrey.

Originally published: Toronto: Anansi, 1967.
Issued in print and electronic formats.
ISBN 978-1-4870-0124-7 (paperback).—ISBN 978-1-4870-0125-4 (epub)

I. Title.

PS8513.O33D4 2016   C813' .54   C2015-906996-3
                           C2015-906997-1

Library of Congress Control Number: 2015954260

Cover design: Alysia Shewchuk
Series design: Brian Morgan
Cover illustration: Brian Parker

We acknowledge for their financial support of our publishing program
the Canada Council for the Arts, the Ontario Arts Council, and the Government of
Canada through the Canada Book Fund.

Printed and bound in Canada

DEATH GOES BETTER WITH COCA-COLA

INTRODUCTION
by LEE HENDERSON

DEATH GOES BETTER WITH COCA-COLA is an unsettling title. For a debut collection of stories, it calls to mind a sweet, effervescent finale. This is Dave Godfrey's first book, and only the fourth published under the House of Anansi imprint he co-founded with Dennis Lee. They launched House of Anansi in 1967 to publish poetry — Dennis Lee's — and Godfrey's own prose certainly shares a poet's sensibility. He's able to amplify through compression, and create vital, urgent life out of rich language and pitch-perfect voice. Rooted in image, digressive in approach, often these narratives progress through unexpected sidetracks. Not every sentence follows the path laid out for it in the sentence before. But in every piece, the writing pulls you along. The stories reveal themselves in peripheral vision. Eventually ideas and images all join, but in the meantime, the language is breathtaking.

The story "Mud Lake: If Any" begins: "Death, too, I think at times, is just another one of our match box toys."

This from a man said to be at least three people in one, "and all larger than life," according to Dennis Lee. *This* from a book about hunting for food, hunting for sport, fishing, drinking, killing, about the Vietnam War, about music, addiction, loneliness, and love. A book about death that downplays death. A book about death levelling death to a universal meaninglessness. As if death resounds no louder than the pop of a carbonated bubble.

I start to think it's true, the grand scheme of things wipes us all away. The universe is infinite and fourteen billion years old and reading, writing, and arithmetic were invented in Iraq five thousand years ago... and yet we each deserve our tetchy little time on Earth. It's not death, time flattens us. Even the infinite universe has an age. At first I thought Godfrey was being sort of blithely ironic throwing away his title on a poppy line like that, but the more I thought about it, especially in relation to the *I ching* hexagram readings that begin each story, the more the title seems level-headed. Funny, a bit ironic, but still true.

Death Goes Better With Coca-Cola splits history into time before 1886 and the years since the beverage was invented. Once that anodyne fizz of a tiny epiphany first broke on lips, all of us were changed. More than any deep connection to the stories, the title is more like a kind of sixties pop art reference, true and funny and ultra modern. And Godfrey's voice across these stories reminds me a bit of Andy Warhol's coolly bemused, passionately indifferent persona in his writing and interviews, where it's sometimes impossible to tell if he takes any of what he does seriously or if any of it is supposed to be funny. There is in Godfrey's prose Warhol's desire to make the bizarre popular and the normal holy.

I remember how in Raymond Carver's last story "Errand" he ends Anton Chekhov's life bedridden in a hotel room with a glass of champagne. Chekhov lifts his head to take a sip. "It's been so long since I've had champagne."

After all, why not a sweet buzz then? Why not a bendable straw? It's been so long. Carver died not long after he wrote that.

IN 1973, six years after publishing *Death Goes Better With Coca-Cola*, Godfrey looks back on his debut collection, in response to the question of coolness from interviewer Donald Cameron in *Conversations with Canadian Novelists – 2*: "Over all it's not really coolness, there's a real desperation in *Death Goes Better With Coca-Cola*. That need for coolness comes out of the desperation, you know. What the fuck is going on? Guys are dropping off all along the way, which is the way it was. When I went through my late adolescence, friends were just dying here and there…"

Two world wars. Korea. Lebanon. Cuba. Vietnam.

"Death, too, I think at times, is just another one of our match box toys. I am now, as the lecturing surgeons say, preparing the electrodes for insertion. I am now, into the alien elements, inserting myself."

"I am now, into the alien elements, inserting myself." What a line.

The narrator is out duck hunting with a friend. The "alien elements" are the hunt itself, I think. The hunt is what remains forever unfamiliar. The "alien elements" offer opportunity and risk. Instead of bringing home fowl, they almost get themselves killed.

The story "Flying Fish" begins, "It is a flying fish I want to catch. I have lived in America for many years and it is strange, I am a doctor of philosophy, but I have as yet never laid hands on that elusive creature." Instead he meets Mr. Goodman from Pennsylvania, a less-than philosophical American, "connected with the corporation," Continental Can, owners of this seventy-thousand-dollar fishing yacht. The trip goes south from there. Godfrey sends his characters hunting only to remind them of how often one must fail if ever to succeed. This story and many others remind me of writer and editor Gordon Lish's statement in an interview that fiction "must speak with the menace of death at hand."

Hunting recurs. Hunting for sport, for food. The hunt might

be Godfrey's subject, but language is the real game. He's on the hunt for that elusive epiphany.

The sentences are singular in every way, but it's also in their unique combination and sequence, and how these lines join in unforeseen patterns that makes his fiction still relevant today. The style and techniques in the prose remind me as much of Hemingway as the literature that came after Godfrey. There's precision, irony, and a morbid formality to his approach that's reminiscent of authors Gordon Lish edited in the eighties and early nineties, certainly of Raymond Carver, Barry Hannah, Diane Williams, and Christine Schutt to name a few. Godfrey sometimes reads like a premonition of Denis Johnson and Amy Hempel, the fiction of lowlifes, drifters, and addicts, with an ironic reverence for the spectre of death, making poetic leaps from one period to the next. Among the fields, Godfrey's chosen only the perfect words for print. Sentences decorate the pages like blue ribbon trophies. Every paragraph is as tight as a horse race.

There is a connection between Godfrey and Lish, but it seems rather more like an affinity or shared sense of purpose than influence either way. In 1965, three years before Lish got the job editing fiction for *Esquire*, he published Godfrey's "Images. Creosote. Beast Bodies." in a literary journal he edited called *Genesis: West*. Opening line: "What do you see from a freight car, when you live there?"

Godfrey includes a weird autobiographical story, about Gordon Lish, in his 1978 story collection *Dark Must Yield*, a cautionary tale called "Binary Dysfunction: Portrait of an *Esquire* Editor." It begins: "He had difficulty determining the shape. It seemed as though it were a shoulder. But at times it felt more like a thigh. It was definitely female; there was nothing exciting to Gordon's life. His brothers and sisters had stolen all the excitement."

It's a gnostic, abstract story set in a lost world, a story following a man named Gordon as he bumps into strange things in the dark, remembers only fragments of his past, lives in a pipe, struggles through a sunken city, and does a deadman's float in the flooded post-apocalypse, concluding with a raving novelist's query letter: "I see you have started Anansi after your African adventures so I am thanking you in advance for your kind cooperation as one who knows of what I speak."

African adventures do appear in *Death Goes Better With Coca-Cola* — after all, Anansi is the trickster spider-god in Ghanaian mythology. Godfrey was a teacher in Ghana and personal experience would certainly seem to shade stories like "Up In the Rainforest," about hunting python near Accra, then hearing a band called The Avengers play at a local bar. As a trumpeter, Godfrey toured the continent with a jazz group and wrote a fictionalized account included here called "Fulfilling Our Foray," about a gig in Kumasi. The location seems less exotic than the prose.

Godfrey found this style early and it's fairly outside the over-large shadow of Hemingway's, though not totally untouched by the influence. There are hunting stories in here, after all, and washed-up men. Godfrey's characters are unheroic and not tragic, just social outcasts, part of a washed-up generation at a loss how to change the world. In a swift four sentences from the story "Two Smiths," Godfrey, like a seasoned reporter or imagistic historian, sums up the entire sixties counter-culture: "Then when Spring came he painted his car with flowers and became more interested in the war and eventually burnt his draft card. He was the second person in the whole country to do that. Events swirled about him. A washing machine millionaire, third-generation, offered him financial support."

Later in the interview with Donald Cameron, Godfrey is asked to consider his books in light of his debut. "I think in *Death* a lot of the pattern of control is literary and imposed." Whereas, of his 1971 Governor General's Award–winning novel *The New Ancestors,* Godfrey sees the "pattern of control is taken from life."

The New Ancestors is a long, experimental novel. Godfrey's short stories are the pace of a pop song in comparison. Their brevity makes experimentation normal — the short story can tolerate a lot of play, the form can pull from the literary *and* from life. Two, maybe four pages. That's all Godfrey needs to take a reader to West Africa, Florida, or Ontario. One could almost recite a few of these stories in a single breath. None of them are too long to hear aloud. Not a single one of them is linear. They go around and around. They walk in truth. The truth is a voice. The voice has gravity. Almost like an impromptu monologue from a master raconteur in a noisy bar, or confessions to a therapist or a courtroom, that's the remarkable, very human structure Dave Godfrey captures in these brief, wonderful stories.

With thanks to Rebecca Godfrey

LEE HENDERSON is the author of the novels *The Man Game* and *The Road Narrows As You Go* and the short story collection *The Broken Record Technique.* He lives in Victoria, B.C., and teaches creative writing at UVic.

For Ellen

KONRAD LORENZ
ON AGGRESSION

The balanced interaction between all the single norms of social behaviour characteristics of a culture accounts for the fact that it usually proves highly dangerous to mix cultures. To kill a culture, it is often sufficient to bring it into contact with another, particularly if the latter is higher, or is at least regarded as higher, as the culture of a conquering nation usually is. The people of the subdued side then tend to look down upon everything they previously held sacred and to ape customs which they regard as superior.

CONTENTS

DEATH GOES BETTER WITH COCA-COLA

THE GENERATION OF HUNTERS

SOUTHERN CALIFORNIA FLASHES constant warnings to you about your body stenches, and ignores its own. In a bar in San Diego, on your way to be interviewed for a job you don't really want, there is always this marine: heavy-fleshed, loquacious, his uniform immaculate, still on top of his liquor, nameless as all Bobs and Jimmies are nameless.

He's been around. He doesn't mind that you're drinking Canadian Club—he likes the ads—but he'll stay on beer. Sure, he knows Kenora and the Whiteshell, anybody from Duluth way does. Man, he'd like to get back there; he's been on a bad detail, for a year, escort for the dead. But it gets him around, it gets him around. Fresh back from Tennessee yesterday. On detail. A punk. Just a punk. Who wrapped his Chevy around a pole on the way to Mexico. After whores. But the body returns home with escort.

Now they're getting some real heroes though, that's one thing you can say for Vietnam. He doesn't have a lot to say for Vietnam; unlike many he avoids the regular terms of hate. When his memory of change within his life comes out it's a neat well-packaged story, an accepted memento; like a St. Christopher medal wound about with Saran Wrap against a time of fear, or simply protected

1

against the grit that enters the cleanest of pockets. He speaks his
story without a slur, with mere traces of a rapid-fire stuttering.

WE HAD ALWAYS been bothered by bears while berry-picking. That
year my father left me with the .306 and just four shells. "Don't
waste anything you don't have to," he said. "You're in a war." ·

That war had been going on for what seemed forever to me.
As soon as it was over I was going to get to practise real shooting
again, instead of just sighting and squeezing. As soon as it was
over, I told myself, a lot of things would change. It was 1943; I was
fifteen years old.

"Take care of yourselves," my father said. ·

Ginny cried some. The other girls were older.

"Don't tire yourself out on the drill floor," my mother said
to him.

Which wasn't what she meant. In late summers like this, when
the blueberries came ripe, we would go to my father's hunting
shack for what my mother called a shit-and-haddock vacation.
"Shit-and-haddock vacations," she would say, "are what you get
when you marry a drill sergeant instead of a pilot lieutenant."

Aunt Virginia had married a bush pilot from Duluth who was
now overseas and sending back more money than enough. She
got around all the bars in Duluth and told tales to my mother.
"What he's drilling during the day," she would say, "may be wearing pants; but let me tell you honey, at night the drilling ain't
through khaki. Cotton, or maybe silk. Midnight black or sintime
red. Better believe it, honey."

Out on the blueberry hills at least we kept to our own sched-
ule. We escaped the driving rages my father brought home from
the drill hall. We escaped the bitterness my mother mortared back
at him. Early in the morning we found a rich area and picked until
noon. Then we went back to the shack for lunch and sorted the

berries into two grades. In the afternoon we would sometimes go
out again for more. Or swim in the river.

With the .306 in my hands, I didn't feel like a picker. I was the
sentry and there were Germans everywhere. Always four of them.
I would get the first three quick, always in a vital. Instantaneous
death. Heart or head for hellshots; legs tor the lazy; stomachs for
sadists. I didn't even know what a sadist was. I was a hellshot.

Except if I didn't pick, my mother drove Ginny and the other
girls something terrible. It was her only way of getting to me.

"Come on, general," she would say. "We need one man, at
least."

I would lay the .306 nearby and pick, with my eyes roving
through the woods like a searchlight. Or so I thought. We weren't
bothered until the Saturday of the third week. My father was due
Sunday morning. The two cubs and the old lady had got halfway
to the big bush we were working on before I saw them. It was
almost like I had planned. I moved off from the bush to keep my
line clear. My stomach was on the moss; my elbows on flat granite. I remembered everything my father had showed me those
years before the war, when he knew the war was coming and
didn't know how long it would last and wanted me to be a hellshot
before shells got too rationed.

I hit the first cub clean, and while the old lady bent over him,
I hit the second one clean. And she roared at that, a sound like a
dog trying to say ground. She came toward the sound of the gun;
stood up on her back legs to see where I was. So I got her in the
stomach. It wasn't where I'd wanted to, but it was where I'd hit
her. I could almost see her pain. Like the first time I'd had beer.
She went back to the cubs and then she went back to the woods.
Loping like a man hid in a gorilla suit.

I *knew* she wouldn't go far, which was my mistake. Because I
could have got her in the head, through the back of the brain, easy

enough. But I wanted to have that fourth shell still there when my father got back, and instead it was a week and a day before we found that old lady. Alone, I lost her even before it got dark.

All that next Sunday my father made me walk with him and didn't say a word, so that I felt like I lived in a house with a stopped-up toilet. Which was what he wanted. All that week I didn't pick because I was sure I could find her, but I couldn't.

And the next Sunday, when we did find her, I found out what my father meant about gut-shots, about stomachs for the sadists. She was in a little swampy hollow. "Any animal goes low to die," my father said. And she was covered with swarms of blackflies; so that trying to see her was like trying to get to your bed in a strange room. My father took out the skull and cleaned it. The stench made me want to be sick, but I knew what he would say. I got the gun ready. For then he did what I knew he would do. He set the skull up at 100 yards and made me put the shell I'd thought I'd saved into it, into the shattering bone and brain matter.

"Sometimes you have to waste something," he said.

When the war was over, my father left for Oregon. "Your mother can look after the girls," he told me. "You'll be okay on your own." I knew I would be.

When Aunt Virginia's husband came home from the war, he was an alcoholic and he died slowly under government care in a VA hospital. The government took care of our needs too, because my father had been a soldier in both wars, even if just a drill sergeant in the second one. I signed up myself in '49. Been in ever since. I guess you must have done your bit a little later?

ABOVE THE BAR where we drink, the big Coors ad, of fireworks bursting across a four-by-three square of plastic night, continues its cycle in many colours. If you have the patience, or the desire, you can figure out the cycle. This next one will be red, you can

say, of the imitation Roman candle that arches its way into nothingness. Yellow. Blue. Green. Yin. Red. Blue. Yang. The sun which
pales. There are times when you seem conscious of observing
inevitability.

AN OPENING DAY

CHUCK WAS LATE because he had been all the way down to New Orleans on the weekend. So I performed our duty alone, by going out on the line-hunt with Vernon and the other farmers in the morning and shaking the pheasants out of the corn. The fields were half-cut, with about twenty rows down and twenty up, so that it made for good shooting, although somewhat mechanical. We walked in a line, as though we were beaters for some rajah who would never arrive. The birds were very well-fed and the older ones, when they couldn't run, would burst out of the tall corn just at the height of the taller stalks and fly there, down the row, or suddenly across, so that the shots on them were difficult.

The farmers were very good at those shots, and they were serious and efficient men, so that by noon all of us had our day limits and they left, because of the filled limits and because the moisture was at a good level for the corn and they all had a lot to get in. If it got too damp they had to use dryers and that burned a lot of expensive electricity.

I ate lunch and when Chuck came we went across the dirt road to where there was a weather-beaten house, once painted a gaudy orange, but now almost penny brown, at the end of a long driveway where the fence was rusty and weak at the corner-posts. Behind the house was a tall, cylindrical crib made of open wire, and still a quarter full of shucked corn, and to the left Inter-state 80, so that the fence there was new and taut, and beyond the single open crib, running east along the new fence, was a row of storage bins, the colour of old pewter, closed-in like inverted mugs, three across and forty long and with many cubits of corn inside each one.

"Let's try around the open crib," I suggested. "If it's good for the Angus it should be good for birds."

Nothing stirred up.

To the right of the crib was a field of timothy and white clover and weeds, crushed by the winds and strong with seed. The field was high in the centre and dipped down on all sides, but most strongly toward us. With the dirt road side it was almost even, but before we could get down into that field now we would have to climb two fences, the second one an old one that ran along what had once been a creek bed, where the field ran its steepest slope. Then the grade curved around on the east side, a little more steeply than on the dirt road side, and sloped one final time to the south, moderately, at the beginning of a long grade that ran down through all of the next farm.

Over there a herd of forty Angus had trampled everything into mud, but in our field there were only three horses, a white mare and two chestnut ones.

"Let's try the crown and then come on down on them once or twice," Chuck said.

"Prego," I replied, but he didn't smile.

"Should have a dog," he said. "One of us should settle down and run a spaniel or two."

The last time I had seen him and Mary they had been living in a third-floor flat on the Via Babuino, seemingly enjoying the artist's life, with lettuce stored in the bathtub to keep it crisp. She had been painting blocked-out women in full primaries, and he translating Montale.

We went over the fence and started up the hill. The storage bins were at our backs, as was the once gaudy orange house. The horses had left shit in the field, but not much, and they hadn't been there long enough to trample all the resting spots of the birds. The two chestnut horses ran into the corner by the dirt road while we were coming over the second fence, but the white mare stood steady until our first shot. It was my miss. And then Chuck's too.

We hadn't expected birds on the way up the slope, for we had been counting on coming down from the crown and hearing the birds running ahead of us and flying only when too close to the fence. These went right over our heads, two whirring hens and a cock, and when they were past the storage bins they made a long glide across the Interstate to the fallow fields on the far side.

"Home safe," Chuck said.

The crown was thick with grass cover. Rich soil. You could take a cubic foot of the field there, the timothy, and the air, and the sow-thistles, and the falling seed as you brushed through it, and paint at just that cube for a month, but you would never get it and it would have changed. It changed as quickly as the sun-glints of a Finnish girl shaking out her hair after pulling off a hat of fox fur.

In a slow curve from the dirt road to the south-east corner ran a wagon rut, and in the clumped grasses beyond that we put up the second cock and missed him too.

"We've been away too long," I said.

"I just want them too hard. You're being pleasant. You've already got your tail-feather for the twerp. Mary was doing a picture of him, you know."

"She never got to see him."

"In that picture you sent us, with Rachel belly-side up in your corn field when she was pregnant. African corn, eh? Not even up to her shoulder. She looked like she had been planted in it and the kid ready to burst out."

"You should have tasted that stuff. Awful. Even after we boiled it all night once. But I remember that photograph."

"It'll be a good painting."

"She's serious, eh."

"Never was anything else."

"Let's try and work up into that far corner. Might have another chance there, if I don't pepper one of his steers."

"Next time it'll be better," he said.

We walked ten feet in from the wagon ruts, making a lot of noise, and when we did get near the angle where the fences met, a hen went up over the sagging board gate, and then a cock.

"There he is," Chuck had said.

"Prego," I laughed. Chuck tumbled him.

"It must have been an Italian bird," he said. "If you knew one more word of Italian, it probably would have flown back to us. Did you see the way he stopped and listened to you?"

We had to shoo away the cattle to get the bird. We went back over the board gate and through the thick timothy. The one hundred and twenty storage bins along Interstate 80 were not quite out of our sight. As the sun hit them from a lower angle they looked less like pewter.

In front of us, across the dirt road, Vernon had a goodly portion of his field of corn picked and shucked out and sitting yellow as nuggets in the wagons and bins.

"You've never seen anything like it over there." I said, "The way one man would put in a whole field of corn with no more tool than a hand hoe and his back.

"The government gave us a house on a hill and I gave the hill

to a gardener of one of the Party bosses and that gardener and
his wife for months cleared it all of scrub and cultivated it and
planted it, with only a machete and a hand hoe; must have been
almost an acre, but all of it on an incline like a dropped ice-cream
cone, and the rains came early and hard, before he had it prop-
erly mounded, and the top of the field was washed clean and the
bottom was silted up and the middle of the field was bared-out,
so that the corn borers got at it and out of that whole field they
cleared no more than six or seven bushels of corn about the size
of your hand."

My pants were burred and seeded.

"Here you know, Chuck, even Vernon's paranoid about the
Chinese; figures they'll attack sooner or later. A Quaker, but he
killed his two birds this morning. Keeping in shape."

Down in New Orleans, Chuck hadn't convinced Mary to rejoin
him, and now he didn't want to look at things seriously, didn't
want me to talk. He offered me his pheasant while we plucked it,
but I said no, we'd share the feast. Rachel would cook the three at
once. With real wine. We continued on the slow diagonal curve of
the wheel ruts, across the empty field of dry timothy, the blowing
seeds, until we got to Chuck's grey Volkswagen and could drive
home.

THE WINTER STIFFS

"**WELL, THEN I** threw them down from the cat. The two that were solid, I mean. Old Carleton Carl we just unloaded him like cordwood and took him into the blacksmith's and piled him up neat in the corner. Some of them men outside had never seen anybody dead like that before, but I just flung them other two down, and they caught them as they could.

"The blacksmith didn't say much, just set to work on the flange or whatever it was I had come in for. 'Not much I can do with *them* until they thaw some,' he said. Sask and old Billy Ball were leaned up against the wall over nearest to the forge. The blacksmith he just hammered away with his back to them. Then there was this belch, you know when the gas gets warmed up in the stomach it has to get out. This belch comes out, and that blacksmith didn't even turn around. 'Just keep quiet you,' he said. 'I'll get around to you in your turn.'"

The Finn laughed when he told it, when he got to that part.

"I'll get around to you in your turn, Ha."

His muscles ripple with laughter. His mouth is a child's moon of red and white flesh and teeth.

But in France they have been saying for some time now that

you can't do character anymore; this is the age of the regimented number, of K, and all that. And it is true perhaps. Even in Ste. Vitale they have all become masters of nausea and accidie, which makes it difficult to deal with those who belch back at our condition. What the writer should do, we all know, is to make a list of some sort, somewhat scientific, but also new and somewhat unusual. The habitual phrases of the Finn, for example:

Breed.

Old Gutshot and his brother Buttshot.

Let's go grunt at the moose.

How'd you like to breed that.

Happy as a Jew in a junkyard—or a Finn in a Swedish pussy house.

Yes, it's about half the moose in Milwaukee I killed like that and damn near all in Chicago.

Your skating rink needs flooding (to a bald man).

So I bred her until dawn.

Two things that won't stick in a beggar's throat: hot pork and a big lie.

Fifteen hundred dollars last year on kid support and alley money and legals.

And God made fifty percent to screw the other fifty percent and keep us all happy.

Breed, bred, and the joys of breeding.

The cuntless cunt-book (for *Playboy*).

And then the fight began. (As in: and I was down in Montana myself once too, and walked into a bar with all those men in sheep-coats, scraped my hobnails where they would do the most good, picked out the biggest man there, and said—here's to Montana, where mountains are big and the men are men PAUSE and it's every sassy sheep better look out for herself on Saturday night. And then the fight began).

Such a list saves you all those forbidden descriptive words: crude, prejudiced, energetic, life-flowing. But even so it is difficult to find the right garbage can for such a person as the Finn. He is six feet three, with his hair brushed down. He will not be crammed in. "I've got eight inches for you too, sweetie," I can hear him say to the lyricists of decay as they attempt to jam the lid on.

"Eight inches for you too, sweetie!" Before he returns to the story of the frozen men, as the Finn often does, perhaps this time starting earlier back, lining her up from a different angle.

"I was thirteen that winter and we lived right in there by Kettle Falls you know, so no teacher was going to be dumb enough to come in for the three of us pike heads. I was thirteen and I wasn't going to waste the whole damn winter so I went off to work in Dirkson's camp, doing the water bucket stuff. And then that one big night it snowed hard everybody but me and old man Dirkson had gone in to town, a thirteen-mile walk, and Sunday come and nobody was back. It had snowed all night, must have been five or six feet down. 'I guess you think you can drive the cat in and clear the road,' Dirkson said.

"There was something he just had to get fixed. I'd fooled around with the levers and he stood there and told me which to push for what and I worked it out. A little grind there and there. I was pretty big for thirteen, five feet eight with my hair brushed up, but all I had to do was follow the road if I could. The snow had stopped. I went cruising along, happy as a Finn you know where, when all of a sudden there's this bump, bump, bump. Like I hit a log or something. And it was Carleton Carl. All broken up like cordwood, neat as could be. Snapped him like dry pine in August, it was that cold. Coconut brittle. So I piled him and went on more slowly, expecting more, and sure enough there was Sask and old Billy Ball. Must have started out all liquored up to walk home before the storm, or in the storm. Doesn't much matter which now.

"So I took them all into the blacksmith's. Sask and Billy I flung down. I can't remember who caught them, but whoever it was they went white a little. It was still ten below. They hadn't ever seen anybody dead like that. Somebody wanted to get a sack for Carl, but I said never to mind. We just piled him up like cordwood in the corner of the blacksmith's. Blacksmith came in and hammered out a new flange or whatever it was Dirkson had sent me in with. With Sask and old Billy Ball leaning in the corner like two halves of a telegraph pole.

"Being ignored like that must have insulted old Billy some, because then he let out a belch at us, you know when the gas gets warmed up in the stomach it has to get out, and it'd frighten a gypsy, but blacksmith didn't even miss a stroke. 'I'll get around to you in your turn,' he said. 'Just take it easy.'"

The Finn laughs when he tells it, when he gets to that part, from whatever angle of vision. His mouth is a child's moon of laughter.

But in Toronto of course, people are more civilized. In the mornings I take my son out for a walk early, before the streets get salted with people. The morning after writing this down there is an old, single woman feeding the pigeons in the Walmer and Lowther roundabout, near where the Eatons had a mansion in another era. Jon doesn't bother the pigeons, but he loves to see them go up and he laughs and says birds over and over again when they are just off the ground and their feathers are flashes of many shades of grey and white. And I let him. But the old single woman who is throwing seeds on the ground for them becomes annoyed as the pigeons rise in their tawdry flight.

"What is he doing here so early," she says. "Why do you let him do that? That's not the right way to raise a boy, to frighten my pigeons like that. My pigeons. My pigeons." She looks as though she would like to fly after them, but Manufacturer's Life has shackled a fifty-pound gold egg to her left ankle. With a silver chain. A thin ankle.

And I, unable to condemn her egg of lonely assurance, I call her lady. "It's a public roundabout, lady," I say. You know that gentle tone with which we in Toronto can say lady, when we mean, really, something entirely different.

IN THE DISTANT SINGING
GUTS OF THE MOMENT

WHEN WE GOT to the cove she dove overboard. The beach was still an eighth mile ashore, hidden from the rest of the lake by a spit of rock and spruce. That beach a boomerang of sand to my eyes, gritty sand of my youth and fears, moving away from us, as we sailed through the cove, in two directions in the same moment: up under the spruce needles withered where the white sand sparkled like salt loosely broadcast over the pumpernickel, and back toward us through the shallow waves, as the eye returns, to where the lake sand ridged itself deeper out of sight below the waters in a pattern of split and loosened pieces of corrugated cardboard. Eighteen, her body nearly fatty, she jumped up on the gunwale, steadied herself there for a moment while the dingy heeled, tilting her body as a loon tilts up his tail before a dive, poising silently until the keel of the dingy had almost broken water, and then she dove deep, away from the overturning dingy, away from my shouts. She came up spluttering and laughing, swam until her feet hit the ridged bottom, and then ran in the waves toward the beach, ran fleetly. Dolphins of kicked water accompanied her.

You'll have a time knowing her again, I thought.

She shook her head and body sideways as her feet kicked up

smaller and smaller spurts of water behind her until she reached the dry sand where she bellyflopped down to let the sun dry her. By the time I had the dingy righted, moored, bailed, and the sail spread full to dry, the sun had warmed her back enough so that she had turned over and was flicking the crusted sand off her body.

"Hand me the towel," she said. "I want to rub the sand out of my hair."

Jesus, let's not talk, I thought. Instructress, how are the old men who lance your moated bum for twenty-four bucks worth of swim lessons? How was your hay fever last fall? How was skiing?

"It's not going to do you much good;" I said, "It's sopping wet."

"Well why'd you do that?"

"It wasn't me, Sara, remember? It wasn't me who made the grandstand play and tried to drown the poor, one-eyed dingy."

"Well the towel was in the bag, wasn't it? It's plastic."

"Yeah, but the bag was unzipped; just hanging there, open to every wave that fickled along. Open to every sailor."

"You can say marin. It's prettier than sailor anyhow. I bet the food's soaked too then."

"The pumpernickel is soggy. We'll have to put him back in the tadpole class until he learns at least the dog-paddle."

"Don't make a mock of me. Is that what we came here for? At least I wasn't always saying I wouldn't be doing it this year. We'll have to eat the herring without bread. We've got to get back early anyhow. You have to play and I've so many things to do I'll go out of my head. I'm really snowed; I swear every bachelor over forty in Toronto's up here poking at my butt and bobbing his head at my breasts when I bend over to show him how to keep his head under right."

"What train's he on?"

"Come on now, I was speaking of vast numbers. Why don't you put some guck on my back?"

"It sunk, Sara. No more guck. Went down with the ship. You'll have to take the sun straight. Old Sol, then old Scroppy. Unless you want me to dive for it; can't be more than a fathom down. I could see bottom when you jumped. Here, I'll get those. Those shoulders must really move him, all brown and soft."

"No, I'll do it myself. You know my shoulders are too big for a girl. I always mistrust you when you say you like them. The guck doesn't matter; I guess I'm brown enough from last summer. I won't burn if we don't stay long."

"You must really snow him, all brown and ripe, even in the winter."

"January seemed the longest. I've been using a lamp since Easter. It never works out as well. Don't. He doesn't worry much about my body; he's like my father. I could get as fat as a horse and he wouldn't care as long as I was happy. He's got different reasons though, he's studying Indian philosophy. He doesn't care about my stuhla because he's concerned with my sukshma; he's really very different from you. I've reformed completely for him."

"With your what?"

"What?"

"What's he only concerned with?"

"My sukshma. It's the body that you feel is your body, the true body."

"So quit not-talking me and come feel my sukshma."

"I knew you'd say something like that. But you're right for once, because the one you've got is the only one you ever think about; though it's really just your stuhla."

"Oh for Christ's sake, let's go sailing."

"Not now, Scroppy. Why don't you tell me about your playing, if the conversation is beyond you. I thought you were going some-place else this summer."

"Did I really ever say that? I must have been conning your

sweet innocence. I'm glad to announce that I've made a new assessment of my revaluations of self in terms of potential potential, so I'm back."

"Thanks, my little father. You said if there was one thing you weren't going to do it was come back up here and play in the pavilion. Minus certain words which are unladylike."

"Why don't you roll over and play dead?"

"You said you absolutely refused to play with a mickey band like that ever again."

"You roll over and I'll guarantee you'll be browner in one day than you were all last summer. Your pretty sukshma too, if you like."

"Come on now, watch it. You said you'd walk into the lake and drown before you played one note for them."

"Brown to the waist, so you'll be more squaw than lady, a nice brown you can't get in the stores, greybrown like a deer, with only your underbelly white too like a deer, and maybe the insides of your ears and a flicking tail."

"I even did get the insides of my ears tanned. Remember it was so damn funny when they peeled in there, I thought I had leprosy. That long week when you weren't practicing, even in the mornings. You were so nice to me after the first time I thought I'd cry. Even Squeaks said I'd cry — but not for that. We used to get here even before the sun was up some times and then just lie here all day in the sun and not worry about people until you had to go back and play at night. That was just real nice. Even the soles of my feet got brown out here and the boss said I must have had quite a vacation."

"One last sail, Sara?"

"No. It wouldn't be right now. Don't make me."

"Is he a good marin?"

"Come on now, Scroppy. That was the agreement. We said not to talk about him if I came out here with you."

"He's a lousy marin?"

"I don't know, honestly. I'm only eighteen now. You know, Scroppy. It's not impossible for me to be pure. He can't tell from the way I act, so he never tries."

"He must be blind. Is he old?"

"That was my mother's mistake, not mine. He's younger than you are. A war baby, eh? Stop it now, please. You should have come to Montreal. There's lots of music there. We went to band concerts and symphonies and the city has its own singers; not just those brassy bars you have to play in, and those dirty cellars. The Silver Dollar Bar."

"I had to stay in Toronto, you know that. Come on sailing, love. You're right, I don't really want to talk about your loves and lives."

"What was it you used to say?"

"When?"

"When you were telling me how you were going to be in Paris this summer, or New York, or India."

"You should never believe a nineteen-year-old boy. I used to say we made a nice old New Orleans band, you and me: two beats to every bar and a nice steady drive towards that last big chorus where we both could get polyphonic to our heart's content."

"No, I never believed that. This was something dirty, and then 'and he really kicked down the stars.'"

"He really blows his ass, he really kicks down the stars. It's not pretty, it's a compliment. The right ones said I ought to go blow first bone for the Salvation Lassies."

"You thought you were doing it all for me, didn't you. You read too much *Ivanhoe* as a boy."

"I did it for you and your stuhla, Sara. That was a mean thing to say, that I only thought about your bod. I worried about what you were thinking a lot; I still do."

"I know. I'm really sorry things got so heavy between us. I'd have liked you to be famous and let me tag along around the world, like my mom did when dad was on the Olympics."

"You have to be paranoid to make it today. Now when your father made the Olympic team, just because no one else in the whole damn country knew what a discus was, things were different."

"That sounds like his kind of excuse. Half a joke, half a lie. I'd hate to think I helped make you not sure of yourself, like he is now. Don't do that to me."

"How is he now?"

"Oh he's better; he's always better in the summer when he can go fishing and just forget everything. I brought him a hundred flies from Montreal, little funny ones with French names and feathers of blue jays and what not."

"Is he still making all those stainless steel things? Those pipes and tubes for Pepsi and those little nuts and valves for the milk companies that cost about forty bucks a throw."

"No, he lost that too. That was his last great deal. I wish you were more sure of yourself; that's all you need."

"One more sail then. That'll build up my potential potential. You must be creaky after a whole winter's layup. We'll go slow as a herd of turtles in a sea of molasses at first, then just add sail slow and slow until you're a bluenosed schooner bound for rum and the West Indies and those hot, blue seas. How's that for assurance?"

"You were pretty sure about me, weren't you?"

"When?"

"When I said I'd come out here today."

"I always said that when a smart salesman gets his foot in the door he's a damn fool if he pulls it out an inch."

"Oh make a mock of yourself, damn you. I brought him those flies in, he looks about sixty now, and he didn't even have them in his tackle box before he started asking me where I got them, how much, who from, did they look like they were smart enough to know what good national distribution could do for them? And he knows he doesn't believe in it himself anymore, that's what's so damn sad. I could hear you laughing at things, but I would've cried if I were alone. They're so strong and so right for so long, and then one day it gets like that. I felt like I wanted to love him back to life or never touch another man again, never raise children; I'm not sure which."

"I'm sorry, love. Let me kiss you a penance."

"I suppose so, I suppose so."

"That better?"

"Maybe so."

"Here?"

"Here."

AND SO THE sail went up once more.

What did I say to her?. Not much wind, baby, give her some jib? Come on baby let's go downtown? Look here, I'm the one-eyed dingy and you're Lake Temagoshka who's going to wash me of a winter's encrusted ice? Did you really see me, when he said, and I can hear him: "I bet I could make a million of these move in the big stores in a month, give me a good tourist season. Did you ever see a Royal Coachman like that? Fine, really fine." I bet he tried to sell his way out of that rest home when he got better, out of the shaved head and the electrodes, out of the look on your face, his little lady, his sweet Sara, that look-I'm-happy-now face that couldn't play poker behind the great wall of China without crying over every unfilled flush. Open your eyes, see me, sweet Sara, be mean to me at least as you were at first when the guilt was toughest. O wash me of something.

She pulls my mouth down to her breastbone, her body moving

like a sunfish on a bobber. Her heart red as a summer zinnia. I too
am eager. My palm on her cheek, waiting for the tears that this
time stay behind the spillway so I drive and harrow my fingers
dry into the damp, stringy bower of her hair and my body burns
as I take the desired, groping, ingnawing measure of her being.

O wash me? Did I say that? Tide. Lava. Sunlight. Kurly Kate
me? Of what could she? Spread some sorrow on me, Sara. Of
the jongleur of performance? As when the walls, when the black
and white table cloths, when the smoke, when the wrought iron
drunks, when the girls with shut eyes and the old men with strong
knees if nothing else, all come in through the silver bell, into
the mouthpiece of silver, into my mouth in exchange for what,
Sara? In exchange for the silver stomping that goes out to keep
them straight up? If you gonna take me my advice, better make
an ugly woman your wife? Could she wash me of that? When I
was exchanging songs with the old men of the strong knees was I
thinking of other times when she and I had gone sailing without
any of these thoughts? In a singing and pure sensuality?

I slap a sand castle under her bum and her green, winter eyes
are open and laughing at me and at the joke of the unspoken prep-
aration I make for her, for us, before the log boom is unchained,
before the trembling, before we reach together snapping at air
with our teeth in the moment of hesitation before we snap at flesh.

And of what did she wash me, finally? For when I stopped
throbbing in my blood I felt laved. When I'm not near the girl
I love, I love the girl I'm near? The nearness of her? The sand
her sweaty brown hair picked up? Those fine sunaged hairs her
belly wore, the burrow her body dug in the sand beneath her, the
scent she transported from an apple orchard in Vineland somehow to this glacier-hewn lake, the timing of her eyes closing out
the sun when she was tired of being happy and wanted to sleep?
The knowing that before she had been as the wind that seems to

come from beyond the circles with the sole purpose of vibrating
our boat with inexplicable suddenness and pleasure like a cym-
bal struck unexpectedly beyond the beat, and now I watched her
limbs tremble with exhaustion and her face powder itself again
with nearly petulant grief and I wondered where was the drummer that would come to dismantle her. Or had I suddenly won
the battle with the loosest of troops? Musicians are like ordinary people; when the job is over they want to go home to sleep,
eventually.

"GO GET THE sail," she said. "We'll curl up and nap on it."

She turns from me and reaches her left hand back up around
for me, for my hand to curl inwardly in the rainforest of her
breasts. You're the boss of this camp, she says and the blood carrying vessels along my forearm laugh and joy at the softness of her
supple and fleshed contentment.

And then there was nothing really for her to wash me of; as
though the act and the acceptance of sleep had not only fulfilled
the need but smashed the fetishes of demand and even their shadows in time gone, destroyed even their records of birth. So I could
feel that some of her old loose happiness was mine and longed to
return it to her, as she had perhaps longed to share it with me, flies
of bluejay and pheasant feathers to outcast her father's misery. I
felt that long-armed joy, that fine-shotted, pure-toned, taut sail
deepness, that elemental melodic strength of the redeemed, that
jointure of tenseness and pride which any good audience leaves
to its jongleur, plus a shade of that cynical joy which comes to
those well-versed in making young dancers come in their fanci-
est pants. Ooo! Went the little girls, ooh! There! Went the young
men, see! There! And if I felt a small letdown when she scurried
away from me to stand silent and more embarrassed than ever
before in the lake waters, it was of nothing harsher than seeing

the dancing-people clutch their coats and depart. Tomorrow they would return. I had a contract again. Get her to come hear me play tonight and old Mr. Sukshma would be out of this union forever. I chased after her into the lake. Dolphins followed me also.

And the water ate at the nudity of her body as though the water were a field of hay riffling and rippling beneath the blossom-casting tree of her movement.

"Don't ever go right into cold water immediately after strenuous exercise," she said. "One's liable to catch polio."

We moved further along the beach, more behind the protection of the spit, before we slept. Not until the sound of the jukebox in the pavilion had crept across the silent lake to us did we awaken.

"Don't be mad at that now," she said. "It's not bad coming from real far away like that."

"It's those damn kids that get there early and can't keep their pants on one damn minute."

Drifting across the lake from another country:

Annie had a baby,

Can't work no more,

No, no, nonononono,

When she starts in working...

WE SANG IT to keep warm as we dashed through the darkening cold water with the sail over our shoulders to where the dingy rode softly at anchor. We sailed towards the light which the pavilion cast over the lake. Her back was to it; she faced the cove.

It would have been cold enough on the lake to freeze my enthusiasm, if sadness hadn't been so obviously overtaking her. If happy lover A is sad, I considered, then sad lover B is perfectly at ease to be happy. She dragged her hands in the water to keep them warm, but I felt no need to imitate her. I handed her the jacket I had stowed and leaned back to watch her with my arm draped loosely around the rudder. I felt as if all the itches and portents of sadness which had bothered me during the early summer of her virginity and happiness were transferred now to her, so that I could lie safe in the calm centre, where virtuousness and sensuality bedded together, and it was she who had to walk out on the street and imagine there was nothing to love beyond sexual advantage, beyond the virtuous battles won and lost. Enjoy, enjoy, she had said all that summer; both when she was drunkenly shaving my head as an Iroquois brave, and when she was finally accepting her decision. Enjoy, enjoy. If I hadn't been watching her face, not entirely petulant in its sadness, I would have flipped the words back at her now. It's later than you think, I would have sung. As my father always says, I would have said, the happiest days of a young girl's life are those just after she's been married. And who can add? (I would have added), that exact note of fear and wistfulness with which he would say that. We drew much nearer to the dock. She sat silently, ignoring my gangling presence, with her mind in what dank mere I knew not.

"A young man at eighteen is at his absolute most dangerous, daughter, you can't trust him;" I said aloud, "when he's learned neither patience nor prevention. Yet here I am, twenty-one, and my danger has not diminished."

"So you know some times he'd like to be eighteen again. Great discovery. Your perception's really something."

"Ah Christ, he's a good man, but he never said a word about the anger of an eighteen-year-old girl."

"That was a stupid thing we did," she said, as if finally enjoying her anger. "I'll always be sorry for that."

The drummer. My hand slips into the moving water. Warmth is simply the denial of cold.

"You'll never be always for anything. You haven't got it."

"You can't expect to shame me too; you've had enough. I'll be always when I want to, and who cares about before. That wasn't perfect; it wasn't even fair."

"We've done worse."

"Last summer was worse I suppose? I wanted you more all the time then, even if my stuhla didn't."

"Oh, come off that dung, Sara."

"Last summer was just great, really. My sukshma and my stuhla wanted you just the same, like twins."

"Like an old lady with toy poodles. Come on, Sara. You get over feeling like that. Call it your body, even your bod."

"I never got over it, even after I met him. That first morning here was so great."

"It wasn't, you know that. Some of the others weren't bad, but that first one was funny. That's all it really was, funny."

"No. I don't know about you. But for me it was like what he calls jivamukti, which means union with the whole world or something. It's the closest they get to the idea of heaven. He gets very excited when he talks about it."

"Come on, come on. Any two kids, aged anywhere between three and thirteen, could have done better out of pure instinct."

"I wouldn't know; I'd only read books before."

"That's better, poke at me for awhile. I was thinking before that I should tell you to enjoy yourself more. You're getting to be sadder than I ever was."

"I really like to talk to you, you know. You've been around so much you really give me a different slant on things."

"Poke away, love. Come on to the dance and I'll show you I'm better in other ways too. Bigger gaskets for a longer ride."

"I've got to get to the train."

"Turn around then; we're at the dock."

"Here? Not this dock, damn it. Then I'll have to climb the hill to the station and be late and everything. Shit."

"Never be unladylike. The happiest days of a young girl's life are when she's swearing at her husband. Take the paddle and keep us from bumping."

"What time is it? You're really cutting yourself off from me. The train'll be here and me in a wet bathing suit and your jacket."

"You said you'd stay."

"I never did. What time is it?"

"That train's always late. Go home, change into something pretty, snow him, then bring him down here to the pavilion and let him see the competition. Kick up your heels. We're going to be good this summer."

"You'd make a worse salesman than my father, Scroppy. Don't push it, eh? I feel bad enough. He doesn't like dancing and you know I wouldn't bring him here. Just play something for me. I'm so late."

I lay in the dingy while she hopped out and tied it up; my back feeling the heft of the rudder, my feet sopping in the bilge; feeling the night air getting colder around me, watching her run across the creaky pavilion dock, whose boards whistled white with that soft patina of silver pine wood attains only after years of winter snow, years of the sun of summer, of its wind and waves. She started up the iron stairway to the road. The wind billowed in my jacket.

"We're really going to kick down the stars, beautiful. I'm really going to blow my ass."

Her voice came back down the hill from the road like the ending of a rock-and-roll record, where nobody can think of an idea for the end so they just play the last phrase softer and softer until the sound man can fade them out.

"I'm really going to kick them all down, beautiful." I said softly. "I'm really going to blow my ass."

"Glad to hear it." The drummer was standing on the dance deck of the pavilion above me, Bobby Grimes, a negro from Hamilton, whirling a pair of drum brushes from his fingers. "Nothing like a little loosening to make a man scramble."

"You just try and keep up with the rest of us tonight, eh?" I said. "You're forever speeding things up. I thought I learned you how to count to four once."

"Sorry, man," he said, "didn't know you didn't get socked out there or I wouldn't have put you down so easy."

He walked back inside the pavilion, swinging the wire brushes slowly, one on either side of his thighs, of his dark-suited, slow-moving body. And cold is simply the acceptance of the need of warmth.

NIGHT TRIPPER

WHEN I CAN, I fly at night, for I dislike the thought of crashing into sunlight. So I arrived in Chicago very early this time and I just walked around, after riding in the airport bus down to the Palmer House and drinking coffee there, because I had so recently done a lot of things which I had enjoyed and I was about to make a visit in which there would be absolutely no enjoyment, and I was in search of a certain neutrality.

Walking around, I did not want to remember Tony Hasper and how he had once been, or to think about the rightness or wrongness of the situation; I simply arranged a few things that had recently happened in a list so that I would have something to say. For that had been the trouble, not having such things arranged, the previous time.

Tony was with his friends on the fourth floor of a tenement in the 50s between Greenwood and Cottage Grove. They were eating a breakfast of corn flakes and scrambled eggs, at a table which was a Bell Telephone cable spool laid on its side and painted in very bright oranges and blues. One of them, who was a photographer and had money, was just returned from a trip to India and there were photographs of starving Harijans in Bihar on all the walls. Some of the prints were still drying. He was a clever photographer and you saw not only the burnt, unresponsive eyes of children whose minds were damaged by malnutrition, but also, next to these, photographs of a Rajput man whose hair was carefully combed, and oiled, and dust free. Another of them, who was a painter, was working on a munitions series, but he was too clever. He was doing paintings, on 4 x 4 poplar, of men feeding Nike missiles, and of the Phoenix system for the F-111B. But he had gone too far; he was too overt. He was not sure of his own art. In the corner of the painting he had printed: *HUGHES: Creating a New World with Electronics.* And over another he had printed: *A QUOTE FROM McNAMARA'S BAND: FY 1962 through FY 1966 sales of arms abroad of $8.1 billion ... 1.4 million man-years of employment spread throughout the 50 states and over $1 billion in profits to American Industry.*

"Is Tony still in the back?" I said.

"Sure man," the painter said. "Did you bring us some bread?"

"With clever stuff like that you should be able to sell all over the place," I said. *"Life* should come and pay five thousand just to shoot you all in your new, creative, underground way of life."

"Your friend is in the back room," the painter said. He had on a green shirt with red flowers and wore white jockey shorts and assumed an expression of great peacefulness as though he had suffered to an extent of which I could never become aware. As though my sarcasm was beneath his notice.

Tony was still in the room that had been a sunroom before they had had to plywood up all the windows and put in fluorescent lighting. On the plywood his own early sunflowers were marred by nail holes and damp and by the peeling of the paint around the imperfections of the board. Tony had a bed and there was a hand-woven rug on the floor.

"How's it going, Ton?" I said.

I looked at him very closely and then I just wanted to talk and I was glad that I had my list arranged.

"I was coming back from the coast," I said, "and I just thought I'd drop by and tell you what it was like."

Doom is dark and deeper than any sea-dingle, I thought. And what cage is like the iron-cage of despair?

"You'd have done some wild paintings," I said. "We'll have to go sometime. It's not exactly the Vineyard, but it's beautiful. And far from spoiled."

And the sea there was omar deep and ephah wide, I thought. But that made little sense.

"I fished a little, but you know how it is—never enough time to get at ease. I was only really lucky the first time. Took a bus right out of the city, not very far up the coast, to a little bay where there were ferries going past—like buses on Wabash. I didn't even want to catch anything there. It's already late May out on the coast. I just wanted to sit there, bobbing, off a little cave that ran right into the mountains, called Hole-in-the-Wall, and that looked like it owned a spirit or two. But I had the herring strips down, almost by habit, and I got a nice Spring. Hard to carry on a trip though, and I would have given it away or something, but a boy with his father in a rowboat down the way got one too, larger, and I decided then to keep mine. I went up to the restaurant over the bay and watched the weather and watched the father and son clean their salmon while I ate some shrimps, and then I went and borrowed their gear to clean mine. They weren't very impressed that I had to borrow gear, but the boy was very proud of what he had caught. The two of them were very short and they looked like one another.

"The next day I went out on the island, but the wind was blowing right down the strait so I couldn't go out. Talked to an old navy-man fisherman for a while and we quoted Pope at one another. *Horace still charms with graceful negligence.* That was his favourite, standing on the boards of the pier with the boats rocking along each side and a small flock of Goldeneyes spiraling high and wary off the far shore. *Horace still charms with graceful negligence and without method talks us into sense; will, like a friend, familiarly convey the truest notions in the easiest way.* It's hard to believe when you meet someone who thinks in that way and still has a memory to use.

"He suggested I might try one of the rivers, and drift-fish it, so I did, but that was a mistake. The river was open, but it shouldn't have been. Not this early in March. I had a good guide, it wasn't that. But there were so many black fish, spent from spawning, that the clean ones you picked up were in your mind tarnished by contagion. I only drifted down for one afternoon and then I came here. Through Seattle.

"Seattle is a bad time now. I had to wait until past midnight for my connecting flight. The place was full of soldiers and whores, as though it were the '40s again, but there was one mess of unsureness in the air, Ton. I talked to them, but I couldn't talk to them about certain things. About the father and son, for instance. And the not talking of it made it almost an image of old calendar art for me. I'll have to take you up there and have you do it modern for me in the summer, when the fresh run comes."

Tony did not reply, of course, to any of this. The switch is off. The grey is monked. His cow took an overdose. This train is full, Charlie. Grass from a lyed mine. Etc. Etc. For more than a year, gentle amateur physicians and readers, he has been convinced that he is a pawpaw tree and its fruit, and says so, with additions and variation, when he talks. If there had been any change, his friends would have told me about it.

They haven't taken him into a hospital. That is what we fought about the previous time, when I hadn't prepared my list and when

I blew up at them after I had seen him. One of the friends is a spoiled social worker, if there is such a category, and doesn't trust the system into which Tony would be placed if they gave him up. They were all with him when he took the last bad trip, although they all pretend to know that it was bad stuff and nothing else that switched him out. They take good care of him. Tony's father was a tailgunner in a bomber. His mother raised him until he was fifteen and then she married her Dreyfus Fund salesman. When I knew him he was in his early twenties and just bursting into a creative life. He was an action painter, and would paint sometimes for five or six hours straight, hurling, scraping, lashing paint onto canvas as though it too were alive and quickened by his own energy. He took peyote the first time simply because he could not conceive of himself as somebody who didn't. We turned it at a funeral chapel, an old, refurbished Victorian house. When he first tried to chew it he got sick and couldn't keep it down. We had to wander around town and find some gelatin capsules so he could get the small chunks of peyote into his stomach without retching. Then he went off and on. At times he could swear I was trying to knife him, or that I was coming at him with an axe, and he would crouch in terror and run away down black alleys; at times he would become euphoric and warble about the blue guitars he was hearing and the tomato skies that embraced him and the vitality of the golden blood he could feel carousing through him and speaking to him of wisdoms. When he came down off the mountain he remembered the fear and he swore never to take it again. For two or three months he refrained and worked on his sunflower series. Then he turned his head to acid and I went to another continent. Now his friends take good care of him. They have seen minds burned out in other ways. They have chosen their reasons; they do for him what they would have done for themselves. Under the circumstances.

Mais moi, I am glad that I have a list prepared, my mind at least roughly organized so that I need not think of old measures, of omars and ephahs, so that I can continue talking.

"If you come out there to that coast with me some time, Ton, we'll go all the way up into one of the sounds and just fish and live on the boat and argue. We'll take about a hundred of the big Ryecrisp cartwheels you can get out there and a sack of spinach for greens. The sea is full of fish for the asking: rockfish, perch, oysters and mussels. And when the spinach is gone we can get our greens from lamb's quarters, sheep sorrel, nettle greens, sea plantain, Indian consumption plant. Or have Labrador Tea on the shore."

This list of things I talk about to an old friend, a man of only twenty-six, a man of whom I have good memories, a man whose eyes are as bleary as any famined Harijan child's, whose face is as without character now as the split globe of a lemon-half, scuffed into an alley's soot.

"If we go up maybe you'll get that for me, the way the two of them looked like one another. Like my ancestral spirits walking up from the sea. They both wore those black, red-soled, rubber boots, turned down half so that the thin grey cloth inside showed visible to the sun, with their red-and-black bush shirts open at the collar to the warmth of the day. And something in their faces, something of a human similarity when they looked at one another. The boy carrying his salmon in his arms like a flopping treasure."

When I finish the list, I simply repeat it, with few variations, almost singing parts of it, gazing at the sunflowers and at memories, at the sun-streaked alleys outside beyond the plywood. Gazing at that great dead mass of flopping salmon as the boy struggled to keep his arms straight beneath it and struggled to be able to assume its entire weight as he moved up slowly from the sea.

TWO SMITHS

MAY. SPRING IS LATE TO COME. Slush and the streets full of shivering lushes near the Spadina LCBO. The boy standing in front of me eager to talk, hair as long as that of Charles Dickens at nineteen, a gold circle in one ear; impetuous to talk, a bright orange and green sailor jersey striped boldly above his Levi Strauss blue jeans, blue-eyed; determined to tell me how it is with him, why he clipped out on the reserves, where he smoked across the border, his smile twisted in a billy-jo, mountain boy way; gurgling out how it was with him when he got to enjoying his brother's enjoyment of killing people way over there in Asia and how it was when he knew he just had to get out, to cut out, because he could see how easy it would be for him to start enjoying the same killing. He, Jimmy Randall Smith.

SURE. JANUARY. Full winter may never come. Rhett Smith is beside me in the midwest, lifting an old .12 gauge out of his flower-painted Chevy. His young man's clipped beard is gone.

"Have to have the car repainted now," I say.

Rhett doesn't answer. His face is tight in the cold, near-winter wind. Something else is bothering him. Something else is keeping

39

him from talking, from replying to my jest about his repainted Chevy. So that I talk, uncharacteristically. Once we have climbed over the fence and are into the corn fields, completely stripped down now, completely ready for winter. He waves at the thin-faced girl with peroxide hair who sits in the Chevy and looks discontented, as though the heat may be suddenly and mysteriously turned off while we are hunting.

"A funny old bird is all that I'm sure is left," I say. "I've almost given him a name. I've seen him three or four times in the whole year. He's got one singular habit that keeps him alive. He flies straight up."

I look at Rhett Smith. I am not amusing him. He's back in the south, or he's back in the county seat, or in the state's capital, in a courtroom under pressure. He is unable to relax, as I can now in the cleared corn field, looking for that one old bird with the singular habit.

"Shouldn't hunt him down," I say, "but you know how it is, sometimes you reach a certain intensity about getting something done. I've got my freezer stocked. He's probably tough, probably full of old lead.

"Put some lead near him myself, one time, doing it the local way: without dogs, just lots of men in a line. We came through the fields six at a time. Twice we peppered away at that old bird. It's a well-analyzed way of hunting, the way you do it here. The birds go up, they go along, or they go away; it doesn't really matter. There's always two or three men who can get an angle on him. Sometimes more if he flies the wrong way.

"This bird seemed to know there was something else. Went up like a partridge into a pine tree. Went up thirty or forty feet. Everybody had a shot at him, more or less. Good business for the hardware store — that was about all. We all shot into one another's shot. It's just not something you're used to. You're used to a long, quick, lean flight. You're used to aiming ahead. A transcendental bird, I guess. A romantic out of place in the pragmatic west."

Rhett Smith is not looking at me.

"They put a lot of pressure on you, I guess." I say.

"Wasn't bad," he says. "Wasn't bad at all. I admit I made a mistake."

I know him, Rhett Smith. In the modern way I know details, facts, histories. Who he stayed with when he went down south for freedom. What kind of beer he drank with the people he stayed with, the Haydts. What Mr. Haydt did for a living. But I couldn't have predicted that he was going to peak out at this stage. Anger and a desire for action were building up inside of him, that was obvious. And some desire for fame or attention. Then he just threw in the whole sponge. Took a dive or got smart. Realized that he was being led astray by forces inimicable to the American way of life. The way you describe him now doesn't matter, the way you describe him is forever relative. I know details about his beard. I know what precise moment of awareness triggered all the actions of the past three years. The thing, the moment, and all that. Somewhere inside the rented farmhouse it sits in a file.

Now, the corn is soggy with the damp that comes when a real cold delays. A rustle. Down the field, a long shot, the old cock is running through the stubble. Smith listens to it, as though it were a distant crow, something distant and bleak. Into the scrub weed along the fence, the wild marijuana? Or a right turn and across the furrows and back up distant stubble?

"Funny all that wild pot up here, so far from Mexico," I say. "We had a good crop this year, but you have to get it at the right time."

"I was never one for that," he replies. There is something Baptisty about him, small-town Methodist, and I wonder why I am wasting this unusual hunting time with him.

It was newspaper reports of a girl being raped in New York which set him going. A lot of people saw it from an office building, stood up, and went to the windows to watch. But nobody did a thing. Apathy, that got to him. Religious disgust welled up in him. Apathy is one of his key words. Lack of compassion. That's what he didn't want to suffer from when he came of age. The apathy that the newspapers and magazines chronicled for him during the '60s. Oil millionaires and rat-infested slums. He was going to do something and he went down to Mississippi.

Where the police beat him up but didn't shoot him. He thought that if he had been Jewish they might have, but he was a boy of German extraction from Iowa. He came back with a lot of stories to tell and decided to go on a hunger strike. He sat in bars and apartments with the young radicals and poets who listened to his stories. He told them how young Haydt's car had been shot up by the police as they drove home late one evening. "Car's getting a bad case of rust there boys," one policeman said. "Better be careful it doesn't spread." Laughing a little. "That been like that long?" the other policeman said about the shattered windshield. "Ought not to drive around like that. Might have to ticket you. You boys better take better care of that car; bet it ain't even paid for yet."

He told all his new stories and enjoyed the response and trimmed his beard a little more neatly and then in the winter went out with three other friends and sat in front of the Federal Post Office with only a tent and sleeping bags and they promised not to eat until they had raised five thousand dollars for people who had been deprived of shelter and amenities during the troubles in the south.

And raised quite a good proportion of the five thousand dollars, although two of his friends quit and Rhett caught the third one eating candy bars one night and would have asked even that one to acknowledge defeat except that he didn't want to have to go through it all alone.

Then when spring came he painted his car with flowers and became more interested in the war and eventually burnt his draft card. He was the second person in the whole country to do that. Events swirled about him. A washing machine millionaire, third-generation, offered him financial support.

Now, he explains to me very seriously where the wild marijuana came from.

"During the war, the second war, they tried to grow hemp in the state because there was a shortage of rope and they felt that anything would grow here. But it didn't do too well for that purpose. It spread all over the place, but nobody cared. The war was over by then and nobody was interested in drugs. Now they're beginning to worry."

We come down to the corner and the bird hasn't gone up. I kick along through the weeds, but nothing happens.

Repetition. The thin thread of reality. Suddenly the cock goes high, still the colours of the sun and the fall in this dull season lingering beyond reason. The bird goes high enough so that Rhett comes out of his lethargy and gets his gun up and bangs off a shot and I am glad enough at that sudden action to forego my careful watching for the moment when the bird must level off, when it gets beyond even its unlearned height.

"Perhaps he's inherited it," I say. "It's a whole new breed to make things hard on us killers."

A glimmer of a smile.

I have been up to the small town which bred Rhett. His father runs a shoe repair shop which also stocks boots and tennis sneakers and slippers. In the front window is a sign which states that one can pay his American Legion dues here. I have been up to the town school from which Rhett graduated and talked to the teacher he says helped spark him towards this life of action.

"Most of the people here are kinda anti-Rhett," she said, with just the smallest of nervous smiles as though I might be weird enough not to understand what was implied, what all Americans would understand was implied. "If not, you just don't say anything. When Rhett wanted to speak on civil rights here in the school last fall, before any of this worse trouble came, there were some who felt he should be let to talk, but those who didn't had a point and what could you answer? We're a public-supported school; we have to walk a middle path. Otherwise you get yourself too involved. My husband didn't want me to come at all to talk to you. I told him what you wanted to know about, about Rhett, and, well, we own a rent house over in Cedar Rapids and we're renting it to Negroes now, but that's our first real contact. I do quite a bit with the Negro in American History of the twentieth century and I was glad to see that this year the English people were reading *Raisin in the Sun* in that magazine they work out of, *Cavalcade*. One of the younger teachers asked me about it, there's a conservative minister or two in town who could stir up trouble if it were handled wrong, but—of course English's different than history—but I told her to handle it just as people. The play was about people in a slum, she said, so I said to her just have them judge it as a family living in a slum and what they would do if they were in similar conditions."

Such is inspiration.

The bird has flown east and landed again in the stubble. We walk slowly up back towards the farmhouse. A light snow is falling. When we reach the fence around the old orchard which surrounds the house, Rhett relaxes and unloads his gun, but I am still alert, the phrases of the woman teacher in his small town still running through my mind. Repetition. I kick through the weeds, walking towards the far fence, and the old cock goes up thirty yards ahead of me. I down him very quickly, before he can do his spiral act.

I offer the tail feather to the blond girl who has been waiting unhappily in the Chevy, but she refuses it. I know that she suspects me as one of those people who led Rhett astray, and we are awkward, so I let them leave and turn to clean the old bird. His left eye has been shot out.

Don Silverbuck phones while I am still plucking wing feathers. He is very excited. He has been following all of Rhett's activities, planning to write another *In Cold Blood* as soon as Rhett is jailed. That is why our house is full of files.

"I'll be home in about two hours," he hollers into the phone. "You should have seen that trial yesterday, you wouldn't have believed it. Clarence Darrow all over again. What a phrase. Rhett was late and he said: 'I'm sorry, judge, we took a wrong turn on the way to the courtroom.' How's that for a title? Sell a million. I've been checking a few things. I don't know how they got to him; he just crumpled. But there's going to be a big protest meeting and all the poets are going to read."

"He told me he got off."

"Suspended sentence. It's a different thing. Christ, what I'm learning about law. They should have let him off completely, that's our point. Or he should have gone to jail. I don't know, something's happened to him. Drugs maybe, I wouldn't put it past them. The FBI were out in force. He's going straight. Did you get anything out of him? We're having real signs printed for the protest."

"No, Don. We just hunted. I'm going to get ready to leave. As soon as they start bombing Hanoi I'm going to leave."

"What? We've got to finish this. It'll make us both rich. We'd never do that anyhow. Bomb Hanoi, you must be out of your mind. Even the generals aren't suggesting that. Christ, we've got to finish this. All the hard work's done; we've got all the details in the bag."

"I shot the old bird today," I say. "Somebody shot his left eye out a long time ago, that was all. That was why he kept going high. That was all."

"Look, you've got to stay. Write a poem, you could do it, and come to the protest. It's all going to be recorded and we'll get some of it on the AP wire. That old woman, you remember, the one we talked to who leaned on the lockers in the hall as though she was going to make them and said please don't repeat any of this, she was there today and she didn't say a damn thing. Just Rhett was a good student, and Rhett went a little astray, but Rhett was going to be okay now."

"I don't know, Don. All you guys are like flies or ants somehow. One of these days somebody's going to lift the swatter and that'll be it. I'll see you at supper."

MAY. THIS MOUNTAIN boy, Frank Randall Smith, walks up a wide and dirty street in my city. He's never heard of Pratt. He doesn't know who donated this street to the city and where the farmhouses used to be, before the high rises, before the grand houses. But he is intent on talking to me, talking about how he got to enjoy his brother's enjoyment of killing, especially one story where the squad had taken three prisoners and nobody wanted to kill them so they dressed the three of them up in uniforms of their own dead buddies, American uniforms, and then let them go a little until the Cong shot the hell out of them. That pleased him to a frightening extent and he is desperate to tell me about it, desperate, while I take him in and buy him a hamburger and some chips and a coke and tell him where he can get a bed for a few nights while he settles into his new life.

UP IN THE RAINFOREST

THE YOUNG ENGLISH engineer, Morley Horstler, was excited to have found someone, even this uncommunicative German hunter, Ure Talle, whose marriage with a Ghanaian girl had worked out satisfactorily. Of course he still had the problem ahead of convincing Christiana to marry him, but Ure seemed to think that there would be no problems after that.

"People leave alone one here," Ure had said.

They were in the plains country beyond Accra, driving slowly because it was not yet dark, and John was enjoying the flagrant death of the sun beyond the plains in the distant ocean. He felt very useful and adventurous. For three months he had been surveying at a dam site up in the forests; before that he had been up by third-class railway, lorry, and camel-back to the desert in Mauritania.

"We have too accustomed become to daytime hunting," Ure said. "To this plan there are numerous advantages."

They drove through the low hills and villages of the coastal plain, past the palm-wine sellers, past trays of red peppers, stacked pineapples, mounds of laterite-dusted yams, the women and girls selling peeled oranges at the lorry stops. The lamps began to be lit for the night.

"Your dam is some effect going to have here," Ure said.

"Their dam," Morley corrected him quickly, angry inside at the habitual expatriate's distinction between the pronouns they and us, not quite certain what it was that really caused these sudden irritations in him. He had been looking forward to this trip.

At Kwangonsi they signed at the police station for their guns and waited for Kwesi Bampong who hunted with them when he was not on duty. They turned off the paved road near a group of mango trees and got set up, loading the guns and adjusting their head lamps. It had rained in the afternoon so that it turned dark enough early for their kind of hunting.

Ure moved off first into the darkness. He was always eager for antelope and seldom came back without one, but tonight he had already complained of the amount of water that filled small depressions and noted that it would keep the main water places sparse of game.

Kwesi went next. Morley felt envious of them both. He could never feel secure in the darkness. It was too simple to feel why the Africans believed in the presence of ancestral spirits. The gutteralities of thousands of frogs were as constant and overlapping as though a new race were looking for its past; the bush babies cried like demented old men; owls were wandering souls. After a short time, his face was a swarm of insects and he switched off the light to conserve the batteries. Kwesi and Ure would pick up anything.

At first, from a distance, they thought the snake was an animal; it was looped down from a tree so that its eyes were at the natural level. Kwesi was the first to notice the swaying motion.

"Good, good," said Ure. "For the bridegroom, power. Virility, you say, hey! Wait, wait. We go close and then you shoot. Put on your torch too. One move at one time now."

Morley wanted to back out, to give someone else the shot, but Ure insisted vehemently that he shoot. Ure calculated the wind velocity and the distance for him; he stood beside him as he shot; he cast a steady beam of light at the python from the miner's lamp on his forehead.

"A very nice shot, I think," Ure said when Morley had fired. "We with our empty hands will not go back tonight. I will have this one skinned for you. And the meat, do not throw away the meat. The meat is very good for eating; is not that so, Kwesi?"

The next day they were back in the city and he tried, as he had before going shooting, to arrange a meeting with Christiana. He began to question her excuses and somewhat angrily she agreed that she would be at the Bamboo Grog Shop that evening.

"My father is not getting any happier about it;" she said, "no happier at all."

That evening, although the Bamboo Grog Shop was festive and the musicians happy and he told himself that he was at home there where the musicians were his good friends, he felt ill at ease and found the highlifes repetitive and knew that he would drink too much and that things were headed for a smash.

Christiana was beautiful and he felt she moved like a river out on the crowded dance floor. She sat down when the Kpanlogo was played, but she danced to all the other dances and it was easy to see that she had been to Holy Child and then abroad for her schooling and that for beauty she was easily head and shoulders above everybody else there. Yet she would never dance more than one number with him, and even when they sat out a dance she would not speak seriously with him and when he tried she laughed about incidents she had seen on her last trip to London or made jokes about the weakness of sterling. Her father was a country policeman, but her uncle was in the Ministry of Agriculture and she was his favourite.

There had been an attack on the Redeemer's life during the week, and no one wanted to talk about hunting. A guard had been killed in mysterious circumstances and Kry Kanaram, who owned half of the nightclub, was convinced that this marked the birth of the counter-revolution. Ure became very happy drinking and listening to the music, but Kry called him a bugger of a German draughtsman three or four times and Ure went home early. He stayed with his wife in the big house which Kry's trader father owned on Embassy Row.

When the Black Stars stopped playing, and the guitar band, The Avengers, had begun, the trumpet player came over to Morley's table. He was a Canadian but he knew all of the band's songs and he played with them except when they were on tour.

"Quite a girl you've got there," he said. "She's been here nearly every night for the last month and doesn't look an inch the worse for wear."

Then the drummer came over to have a drink with them. He was a supporter of the Redeemer and insisted that everybody drink toasts to the failure of the attempt.

"No whitey's bullet will ever kill that man," he said. "Never, never."

The drummer had played for many years in America and took Down Beat and kept up on things. He was very happy because he had been playing well and many dancers had come up during his solos and placed ten shilling notes on his damp forehead. He had a towel around his shoulders like a tennis champion.

The Avengers played for a long time before the Black Stars returned.

"That old music is all through," Kry said when they started again. "These electric guitars are the real show now." He was quite quietly drunk and his thoughts weren't connected. "Where did that Ure go? I called him a bugger to his face. He beats his wife you know. You Europeans are all the same. I found out about that pretty gal, by the way. You make violence your god and then you cry shame! shame! Bloody Savages! when somebody tries to assassinate the Redeemer. Kennedy's death was totally natural. Look at the eighteenth century in England. Savagery. I let that Ure know he could stay for a week once. Big house, you know. Eight bedrooms. But he's been camped in for a month now. Almost two months. He'll have his wife's family there first thing you know. You won't have any luck with that gal. Her uncle's arranged an import licence for Christmas biscuits. They offered us a share, but we declined. Last year there were none and this year you'll have to go into high gear to get over them in the streets. The Redeemer must have taken a fat share. You're too violent, that's all. She'll never have anything to do with a European. Want some real whiskey to drink? I brought it back from Togo last week. In the bottom of fishing pirogues. Seventy bob each."

Morley left while Kry was going to a back room for the bottle of real whiskey. He felt in genuine despair about his situation; it was a case of collapsing or of causing some rash unpleasantness, and neither of those were what he had hoped for this evening. He thought in the morning he would take the python skin and go back up into the rainforest and get to work. Then when the skin was dried and could be rolled up he would have it delivered to Christiana. He would have a record of himself made, a record of himself singing a Housman poem, for he had a good tenor voice, and he would send that to her also.

He felt that logic was somehow slipping away from him, and yet he knew that if he were ever able to read her scattered letters of the past three months, without weaving his own yearnings into them, well then he would be able to logically chart his life up to this moment of thick-headed despair. He told himself so as he drove home.

He had no key to the house and stood there by the door for a long time, thinking of Christiana's letters and considering sleeping on the grass in the roundabout's circle of frangipani trees. But the watchman came up from the servant's quarters with a light and rang a bell somewhere inside. Ure's wife came down to let him in. "You too are drunk," she said. She led him into the living room and turned on one lamp. She was wearing a man's red smoking jacket and while he stood there, blinking in the sudden light, she loosened the ties and revealed her body to him, welted and cut in manners he could not comprehend but strangely beautiful to him, as though she belonged to a tribe which was ashamed of its identity but had to mark that identity; and without words, with the bare movements of her body, she convinced him to make love to her, and he did, and he had never known he possessed such brutal and clambering lust.

When he awoke it was with a start; there had been a sharp click and there was a light on in the kitchen quarters. Ure was standing there in the light from the refrigerator. He was pouring himself a glass of water from one of the many jugs. The python meat was stacked on plates on many shelves, clean and white, like bleached salmon steaks. Ure closed the door and came towards him. Morley looked about himself groggily, but the woman was gone, the light was off, and his nakedness was covered with a coarse Mopti blanket of goats wool. The light in the room was coming from the early dawn.

"I do not think you are well," Ure said. Except that as always the word think came out as though it began with a harsh, sibilant z. I do not zink you are well.

And in the morning it did seem he had contracted malaria, for he was weak and feverish. He had to be driven back to the dam site, for he insisted on moving, and the Italian doctor there chided him for not taking his Daraprin regularly. No matter how much he insisted that he had, the doctor would laughingly repeat his conviction that modern science no longer made mistakes and would stand over Morley as the patient swallowed the bitter, yellow, Chloroquin pills which were to cure the malady.

FLYING FISH

IT IS A flying fish I want to catch.

I have lived in America for many years and it is strange, I am a doctor of philosophy, but I have as yet never laid hands on that elusive creature.

So I have presented myself at the Pier 66 Marina in Fort Lauderdale on the west shore of the Atlantic and I am repeating my phrase to the captain of CALL GIRL.

"It is a flying fish I want to catch, sir."

I do not mention my doctoral degree, nor my feelings about the name of his boat. One does not change me; the other is his right.

I am not wearing sunglasses, a Palm Beach hat, a 35mm camera, although I possess all of these; I am very serious about all this fishing business. The captain and I have already made our arrangements.

"I'm sorry you don't enjoy the name," he says, "but none of us own our own boats anymore. The corporations have bought them all—because they can afford to with the tax loss and all. Mine's Continental Can's."

"It's a beautiful seventy-thousand-dollar boat," I say, realizing how inane that sounds and how inane I now look in my French sunglasses, my white Palm Beach hat, my Leica belly, my green tennis shoes. I do not comment on his phrase, although I long to take a slide of it. Mine's Continental Can's. "That's not exactly true what I just said;" he says, "there are still two owned by people, but they're having a bad time."

"It's just a flying fish I want to catch," I say.

"Sure," he says. "Sure." He does not look at me strangely. "And if you don't mind, it'll be cheaper for you because I'm bringing along another fisherman. Actually you can't mind because he's connected with the corporation somehow and he has to come if he wants."

But I do not mind. Mr. Goodman is from Pennsylvania and he is not a Quaker, nor is he a Jew, nor is he Amish. But he is very active. Before we are out to the buoy he is already jigging more actively than is the mate for our fresh bait.

"Fresh bait is so much better," he says between jerks. "So much better."

"I am Mr. Goodman," he then says. "From Pennsylvania. I am fifty-seven. I have one son in the arts, a professor of composition and theory at the New England Conservatory. I have one son in charge of jet engines for G.E. The arts don't pay much, do they? I can't see why they can't draft all the motorcycle hoodlums instead of a genius in charge of jet engines, can you? How do you like Florida?"

"It is only for a flying fish that I came here," I say.

"I'm after swords," he replies. "You don't have to ask my questions" he says, "but of course, since you can't, I get first chance at the harness."

I am willing. That's where he is mistaken. My feet are shadows. I am willing to give him first chance at the chromium chair which is attached so securely to the floor of the boat. A side chair

will do for me. I like to feel the bait down the fathoms. I can
remember hauling a thirty-foot shark alongside a pirogue in the
Gulf of Guinea long before daybreak with only five Fanti fisherman for my guides. Mr. Goodman can not. Life is easier when you
can help others satisfy their envy of you by silence.

Neither of us catch anything.

"We should have come a week earlier," Mr. Goodman says.
"The run is over."

"I'm sorry I couldn't," I say. "But I find Florida unbelievable
anyway. It is not just all the old people driving around looking
for a Howard Johnson's to die in. It is not just the young eating
Krystal Hamburgers. It is not the miles of clean white boats. It is
not the total lack of Fanti faces in the streets or shops. I did buy
in Palm Beach as advertised: *Articulated figures as carved by French
prisoners of the Napoleonic wars in British gaols out of beef soup bones,*
but it is not that. Not even Fong Sha Noon's—Home of the Chinese Smorgasbord. It is something ineffable, absolutely ineffable,
and I do not apologize for my diction. I do think, though, that you
have a Turtlecat Snapper on your line."

But he does not agree.

There is a distinction between a marlin and a trash fish: a bottom fish, a Turtlecat Snapper, a monster fish. There can only be
marlins on his esemplastic line.

When we are docked the captain rolls the ocean in after us
and plucks me out a flying fish before releasing the ocean.

"Thank you most kindly," I say. "This has been a most memor-
able experience." The fish is already gutted and stuffed. It, in fact,
seems made entirely of polyfoam with the exception of one fin, but
I am rather too polite to complain. "It is something to mount on
my wall," I say. "It is something to always revere and be in awe of."

These are the most pleasant aspects of fishing, I think: memories and mementoes of such a nature. I decide that I will just add

a toque to my outfit next time I go after a flying fish. These are the times when I love the world, when it can be simplified like this. As was Florida simplified from the swamp and the sea.

FULFILLING OUR FORAY

IT WAS GAMALIEL HARDING who brought back the biggest trophy from that trip. I caught malaria. Theophile Karamm grew a heel blister the size of a guinea-fowl egg.

But Gamaliel, who had backed down and wouldn't dare run his Land Rover up north (it's *tooo* hard to get parts now), Gamaliel who made us take Theophile's red, Toyota jeep up into the arid bush (after one thirty-mile return jaunt to recover his sleeping pillow), Gamaliel who is probably the only African drummer to have played with Charlie Parker, Gamaliel the pure socialist brought back (eventually) an object of worth and beauty.

Theophile was of the third generation of Lebanese traders, reared in Britain away from trade, safari-minded. He wanted an African elephant—no matter how strongly Mr. Marx's black cameradoes were fighting to prevent him.

So we went right into the bush, far north into the bush up a trail that near the rare villages would be no more than a path through the maize, to a village that seemed at the end of the line, whose mosque was not even a mud one but a keyhole of riddled logs on the dry earth, a lightly raised pattern on the bare rug of the village earth—earth far from Medina.

"That road he be France," said John Yarro, our guide.

Theophile had selected him and set his first duty: to direct Gamaliel to Lagadouga, where Gamaliel had been told he could obtain a true African xylophone, tuned to the proper mode, with calabash gourds as resonators.

"France, you lazy bugger," said Theophile, "you mean high-up Volta. France he be civilized. But I thank you, my friend. If ever I want to make a dash out of here, I'll know where to come. A dash clean into more of America's strategic space. Very good, Branansi, now where's Lagadouga. Which road be him, John Yarro?"

John Yarro smiled and pointed out a track, running west, and Gamaliel left along it, in the Toyota. Theophile waved goodbye as though he didn't expect to see it again. "Watch out for my capitalistic tires," he shouted at its red back.

"Gawd, if there's a prize for slipshod, we'll be awarded it," Theophile said.

We began the hunt early the next morning. John Yarro directed us, wearing an Olympics T-shirt and bearing Theophile's borrowed rifle. No firearms were permitted down in the capital, or in any of the large cities, because of the Redeemer's fear of CIA plots. We had stopped in a northern market town and borrowed two guns from an old trader who remembered Theophile's grandfather and thought us mad, although he was too polite to say it. He also lent me an old pair of canvas boots. Theophile put his trust in black riding boots.

I bore that shotgun and consoled myself with the thought that the white grandfathers, between 1880 and 1910, had destroyed two out of Africa's three million elephants and that, in the best of times, there had never been many in this part of the continent. It was difficult to think of a reason why we were there; all I felt was thirst and that something absurd was going to happen. We were headed for a river.

I don't know if Theophile thought we were really going to find something there or not, but he walked well. We kept to a trail and he walked steadily. The land was dry and crackling. I could only recognize a few of the trees. They were all stunted. At times birds went up from them, and up from the dried grass, dust-coloured birds, but we ignored them. We must have walked fifteen miles before we came to the river and we had talked little. John Yarro had explained where he had learned his English—on the coast in Takoradi when he had been a chainman for a surveyor crew. Theophile mentioned conserving the water several times, but drank most of it from the canteen. He enquired of my feet. We arrived at the river after about three hours of walking and saw at once that there wasn't enough water around its rocks to fill a sponge.

"What the bloody hell," enquired Theophile.

I was thinking of the twelve or more miles we would have to walk back. I took off my boots to stuff them with grass.

"There's not enough water there to rub down a Mini," Theophile stated. "There'll never be an elephant there in your life. You've been watching too much cinema. Idiot."

"Come off it," I said. "You'll frighten Samba away."

But Theophile was seriously infuriated. He always spoke to his steward and driver as would a Sir Willoughby Patterne, but now he was unusually harsh. It was as though, after the generation and a half of playing cricket and smoking French cigarettes, unexpectedly, a bolt of Manchester mammy-cloth had been dumped into his hands; mere cloth instead of the long, long-awaited ivory tusk, the blood dripping tusk. John Yarro didn't cringe, nor did he reply; until finally, quite a while after Theophile had called him foolish, he blinked his eyes and replied that in two or three moons the elephants would come there in multitudes.

Yes, he said that; I wrote it down when we got back.

"Oh, no master. You be completely wrong. Two three moons he go come here plenty."

Moons.

When I had finished stuffing the canvas boots with river grass we started to walk back. Once John Yarro dug down about ten feet into the earth and came up with a liquid-bearing root, white and sweet. But still our throats dried down to our stomachs. When we came within a mile of the village and passed a girl bearing a gourd of muddy water we drank it.

We came back along the trail the surveyors had made, before they had taken John Yarro down to the coast with them.

I lay under the baobab tree the rest of the late afternoon, the baobab tree of the chief, who sat there also with his wife and a granddaughter of about two. The granddaughter was suffering from kwashiorkor and no one of us moved to stop her as she stuffed her mouth with small handfuls of the dirt on which we sat. From time to time the chief leaned over and attempted to interest her in his hand hoe, a small rectangle of metal fastened to a root carved into the shape of an old man's curled hand. She showed no interest and cried when it was time for prayers, when the holy man came from his house and faced the far distant holy places and prostrated himself in the sandy dirt on which the key-hole of riddled logs formed the bare outline of a mosque.

The next morning I went out early with one of the real hunters of the village and shot a young antelope before the sun became burning. The hunter had antelope feces tied to his old British Army shirt and we didn't go far from the village. Then he put me to shame by showing how he could kill a monkey eighty yards away in a tree, while something kept me from even desiring to aim at the absurdly dancing, chattering, swinging family of the hunter's victim. There was a lovely white pattern to the brown fur of the monkey he had killed, but he built a fire as the day warmed and singed off the pelt deeply so as to preserve the meat against the day.

We shared the antelope with the whole village, feasting on it and on pounded greens prepared as is the fufu of the south by constant and rhythmical strokes of a woman-size mortar and pestle. And that evening it began to rain. Gamaliel walked in four miles to get us because there was a stream he couldn't cross. He had the xylophone lashed to the top of the jeep and was afraid of jostling it.

The jeep's tires fell apart before we reached the Spanish trader's town and we had to have it towed in. Of course there were no spares and we left the jeep with the trader. Theophile later arranged to have the xylophone shipped down and some tires smuggled in. He and Gamaliel rode in a taxi the 150 miles back to Accra and fought each inch of the way.

I left them at Kumasi and rode a lorry into Cape Coast. The malaria had me by then and struck me badly when we got to Abidjan, but that was on another trip, with Rachel, where we didn't pretend to be on safari but went third-class up into Ivory Coast and enjoyed ourselves through Bouake and Bobo-Dioulasso and Sikasso; and when we got to Bamako in Mali and were settled into a small hotel where they kept two tame antelope on the second-floor balcony that ran around the inner court yard, we made love, and afterwards I told her about how the three of us had been bitter on the trip down, with the rain leaking through the roof and dripping the dye from the native blankets wrapped around the xylophone down onto our faces and turning them indigo. I with the first signs of malaria, and Theophile with a huge blister from his riding boots, and Gamaliel happy with his instrument but uncertain as to how he would use it, I suppose, in the city where people distrusted him because he spoke so much about African personality and where the young people all followed The Avengers, whose electric guitars had been purchased for them by the Minister of Defence.

MUD LAKE: IF ANY

DEATH TOO, I think at times, is just another one of our match box toys.

I am now, as the lecturing surgeons say, preparing the electrodes for insertion. I am now, into the alien elements, inserting myself. My colleague, gentle Nye, will observe the reactions of the patient, if any. If any?

The duck boat has been swamped, almost suddenly. We are clinging to its metal sides. Cold; somewhat reassuring. Beyond us and around us, when we have recovered from the shock, from a frightened awareness of chill waters to which we submit not, there appears one of those dinky visions the times are wont to grant us. The Sporting Goods Department at Simpson's, struck by flood, floats toward shore: six wicker goose decoys, a worn pair of oars, one green Alpine tent, eight hand-carved mallards with their neck-wrapped anchors, two arcticdown sleeping bags, a box of Cheerios, my ragged lambswool vest, a soggy blue duffel bag, Nye's insulated pants and jacket of cross-hatched nylon, a spare pair of sole-up rubber boots. Lo, the affluent surface of things.

The waves are gentle. The water not too cold—for mid-September near Flin Flon. Shore less than a mile off. We can push it in thirty minutes, *je me dis*. We bob beside the camouflage-green boat, two anchored heads, and observe one another. A perfect layout of decoys, *je me dis,* if one wanted to call down some passing, strange flock of honking department stores, a migrating flock of Sears-Roebucks, Eatons, Fitchs, Saks, Morgans, Simpsons, Magnins.

Except who then would be the hunters? What highball could lure down such monsters? Nye and I are both submerged to our shoulders. The guns, the ammunition, the camp stove, all things of solidity, are already at the bottom of Mud Lake. Amidst this absurdity of floating paraphernalia, buoyed by their still water-proof lace of feathers, float the one single redeeming object, our afternoon's booty of mallards and coots and buffleheads.

It has been, so far, an unusual voyage but not bizarre.

Relying upon childhood memories of a far more southerly portion of Manitoba, I had blind-guided Nye, a fellow trumpet player and sojourner in Iowa, a veteran of African campaigns, on a long, long trip up beyond the 55th parallel, beyond Snow Lake, beyond the cessation of roads, to the inlet of Little Herbe Lake, to a perfect, marshy river mouth, untrampled by even one other hunter, and as fat with ducks as is a Christmas cake with sweet rinds. It was almost too good a spot, the kind one should visit once and then leave, letting its memory remain to alter and modify your impression of later places both mediocre and uncommon.

So we did only visit it once. It was no regular trip up Little Herbe, and we had progressed as much by intuition as by map-knowledge. We came back down below the 55th (and thus south of the early season), to wait for our one afternoon of regular-season hunting. Off a rock ledge, in deep, clean water we did get some pike; and we thought we might get some Canadas. At night-fall we could hear them, high, high overhead.

Down off the road from Flin Flon to the Pas, we found a

suitably ugly lake, with a harsh, muddy, cat-tail shore, and spent the morning getting our gear through the two hundred yards of shore mud and crossing the lake. Shooting opened at noon; we had a good afternoon, and set off back across the lake.

I'm not sure why the boat was so loaded. Whether we were afraid of theft or had developed a possible plan of spending the night on the far shore and then driving night and day back to Iowa. But loaded it was. I was scanning the shore with Nye's monocular, looking for a break in the shore mud, when I realized that the waves we had been moving through had slowly been attacking us, gently but progressively spilling over the bow, sloshing into the bottom of the boat beneath its mask of gear. I moved back as soon as I could get my legs untangled, but it was too late. We had made our mistake.

I must have scrambled, because the monocular never showed up, but I don't remember being frightened. Nye responded to some pre-imagined plan and freed the motor before we swamped. I stated that we were in trouble, but I was only thinking of wet-clothes trouble, not of the *aglaecean*, hungry water-monsters with which in childhood old trappers frightened me. No mile-long pike troubled me.

I watched our bobbing gear spread out and move ridiculously towards shore, and that expressed our destination. Never leave the boat. We would hang on, and kick behind its stern — our cam-ouflaged, water-heavy, turtle board. But first we had to rock as much water out as possible, and it was on the recoil from one of these foundationless heaves, pushing against the elements that melt away, that I hit the Leacock bottom of that muddy, ugly lake. It oozed beneath me, an ooze of treacle and slushy cement. Which did frighten me. I thought of sinking-sand. And I laughed, rather loudly. Once I had my footing.

Nye turned full-face to me. And I saw, laughing, thinking

really only of Lake Wissanotti, that Nye was truly frightened. The *aglaecean* were taking teeth-sharp bites at him. I remembered then, back in Iowa, his wife bending across to warn me that Nye's response to penicillin was lost in the war, that for him pneumonia could have no sure cure. And he had his hip boots on still, ready for the shore mud, not for this quick calamity. Or say that the German mine was finally tripped beneath his ambulance still rambling across the Sahara, and, wounded and thirst-wracked, he could see the whole muddy lake as no other than a tongue-split mirage.

"Hey, hey," I said. "Bottom. It's the old muddy bottom. Get out the bread-balls and we can bob for suckers."

A mile from shore, we were only neck-deep from bottom. And he laughed too, letting go. Welcoming the mud.

We became surface-floaters again. Collected some of our decoys and protective clothing. Spread by the waves, and soggy, it had lost some of its absurdity; still we let much of it go. We turned down the chance to practice an enforced economy; we dried the gear in the sun and by a fire and slept dry.

Nye knew his Thoreau better than I. "Minks and muskrats," he mumbled. "We go from the desperate city into the desperate country and console ourselves with the bravery of minks and muskrats."

In the early morning, long before sunrise, there was a single shot.

"Poachers," said Nye, mocking my Englishness.

"Somebody who really lives here," said I. "Probably that old Indian who bummed the smokes. Potting a fat hen for Sunday dinner." Said I from my arcticdown, mocking something else, something to do with my own sense of most questionable survival. Was it not my true ancestor who had fired the single shot?

It is one of the strangenesses of youth that you can treat a specific chance of death with no more care than you'd give to your old Dinky Toy, that one-inch, green-camouflaged, British Army troop lorry.

OUT IN CHINGUACOUSY

HE LEFT SHAD lumbering around outside in the top field while he went into the kitchen to greet his cousin Albert.

The hearth was bricked-in and the room smelled of oil heat.

"Not much going or I'd go out with you," Albert said. "Might try back near the tracks though."

Albert had the *Star* spread out on the kitchen table and was exploring the latest adventures of Colonel Canyon.

He felt there was something he should say to Albert this day, but it was winter and there were no crops to comment upon, and his cousin just sat there reading, with his hair rank over his forehead and the blue metal breakfast plate pushed to one side and the blue metal coffee mug glued to the centre of the plate by drying, hardening egg.

"That used to be some house," he said when he came out and had walked with Shad past the silo and into the far fields.

"It is pretty big." Shad had a careful and polite manner of expressing himself, which some people mistook for deference but which was really his way of reaching out. I've worked myself out of something pretty hard, it said, something which you don't have to know about but for which you are perhaps partly responsible.

Although I won't mention that responsibility. It's your word. I've paid my dues. I won't go back. I'm no Bobby Washington; I won't do anything careless. But I'll always be careful talking to you. It said all that.

The front part of the house out in Chinguacousy was unpainted: hasn't seen a paintbrush since the Boer war, as his father used to say. There were no curtains on the side windows, the shades were torn, and you could look straight inside, to mustiness, the falling plaster, trash, rain-stained mattresses. The boards were the colour of long-unpolished silver. Albert lived in the back section, which was low and made of brick. He had burned the ivy off one fall afternoon and the brick was pocked and crumbling, as though it were made of sandstone and not the good clay of the region. There was a C cracked almost into an O on the kitchen window.

"It's a pretty big house, if you consider both parts," Shad chose to say. "Has he lived there a long time?"

"Born there. Bred there. Schooled there. He and his father. My great-uncle and his grandfather. And their father before them."

"You're lucky to know all that," Shad said. "About your family. It must be a lot of work to keep a place like that up."

"Depends on what you're interested in," he said. *Tritavis.* An honourable man knows the great-grandfather of his grandfather.

They went through a grain field that had been partly ploughed under for winter wheat and partly just left to rot. There was a thick aisle of weeds ten feet out along the right fence.

"He's going to have a field full of tares next year," Shad said.

"Vetches we call them," he said. "In case you're ever out with farmers. Watch that one now."

The rabbit came out almost at their feet and slipped over to the seeded furrows. He lifted and let it run until it was beyond damage range; hit it; caused its running to cease.

Shad still had the .22 cradled in his arm.

"Better make sure you're on my side when the riots start," he said to Shad. He felt embarrassed with the small, brown body of fur when they reached it and he quickly stuffed it into the bird-fold at the back of his jacket. He put in a new shell. The lightest of bird shot.

"We'll clean it at the car," he said.

They went over one of Albert's fences: old cedar rails, straightened from their former snaking flow, with a single strand of barbed wire running along the top rail.

"I guess you have to shoot them in the back," Shad said.

"Back? Ass is the word. Sometimes they run towards you. Not often. Or circle. Or cut in one direction. Mostly it's just straight away from your danger."

"You want to do it at this fence?"

"Coming back; if you're still certain. People are usually careful going out."

"It seems funny, but I don't think there's another way. But I'd rather do it myself."

"It'll look a lot less suspicious if I do it."

They hunted.

At the same fence, coming back, with four rabbits weighing down his jacket, he prepared himself to break the rules, the hard, the long-learned, the defensive and inbred rules. But it was still awkward and not easy. He sent Shad over first and passed him one gun. Then he pushed the safety off on the Beretta and flung one leg up on a rail and then the other leg, balancing, and tipped the barrel over the single strand of barbed wire, while Shad stood there passively, almost ready to laugh; and then awkwardly, when the barrel swung downwards, holding the gun as far from the earth as he could, calculating the pattern, he jerked the trigger, putting on all the grip he could with his right hand and using his left as a restraining block to keep the barrel aimed true, although the recoil was strong with no shoulder to absorb it and the gun fought to break out of his hands. Then he looked at Shad, who was laughing now.

"That'll teach you to stay out of my watermelons, boy," Shad said.

"My line," he said. "My line." And laughed out some of his own uneasiness. "Are you okay?"

Shad kicked his foot at any imaginary football "Sure. Should have taken a few extra bennies; but it's not as bad as cleats. I was thinking of that night Bobby Washington shot the marine. I was expecting something worse."

"I was too." But he could not laugh.

He pushed the button on the shotgun and smoke wisped out as it snapped open. He tossed the spent shell on the earth. And he thought of Bobby Washington coming back into that midwest bar after the marine had laughed at him and called him a nigger-girl who didn't know enough to wear a skirt, and had offered to fight him right there or out in the alley or on the sidewalk. And Bobby walked out and the marine laughed and joked about what a real woman could do for Martin Luther, and strutted a little, until Bobby walked back in with a pistol in his hand and didn't even call out to the marine but just shot him six times and the marine never even got a chance to turn around and see what was killing him but all six shots entered his body within a small arc circumscribed from the point where a line joining his kidneys would intersect his spinal cord.

The ground was not totally firm beneath him and he thought of those immense dislocations of his youth, when a voyage of five or six miles would make him vomit as the world beyond the bus seemed to fade away into nothingness on all sides. He thought of McNamara sitting on a swivel chair in the Pentagon and answering the questions of the American clergy. "You know, there are two ways to kill a man. You can kill his body, or you can kill his soul. I'd rather kill a few thousand bodies than kill fourteen million souls in Vietnam." He took aim at McNamara, but he kept swiveling away from him and presenting his back and all of a sudden he himself was the marine and Bobby had come through the door and he knew he would never get to finish his beer and then he was just a monkey in the hand of Buddha, a wild monkey with an Italian shotgun in his hands and a feeling of bitterness that the shotgun wasn't engraved in gold.

He laid the gun on the cold-hardened earth and slapped reality back into his face.

"GOT SIX, EH?" Albert said when they came back to the house.

"Five. And one Shad. I did the real city boy thing at the fence. Shot him in the foot passing over the guns."

Shad held out the boot as though he were some sort of travelling salesman or they were all actors in an early comedy film.

"A little birdshot's good for the soul," Albert said.

He took them inside and Shad unlaced his boot. The foot was bruised and sweaty, but the boot had absorbed most of the damage. Some of the shot had gone well through the tough leather, some taking blue wool from Shad's sock with it so that odd threads curled up like hairs, and pellets were visible as darker bodies within the flesh.

They phoned the doctor and left Shad alone in the kitchen.

"Hear you're thinking of moving into the country," Albert said.

"Charlie tell you? I'm always thinking of it. I hear you've put a price on this place."

"Considering it. Want to see around?" They moved out of the brick portion of the house into the old, frame, two-storied section

and walked through the musty rooms. Old mattresses lay on the
floor; a cracked wash-stand; cardboard boxes and pile of newspapers. The walls were stained. The wallpaper's floral pattern had
been bleached out by time; the torn shades kept out little sunlight.
The fireplace was full of settled ashes.

"Used to be a hotel didn't it? A stopping place?"

"Oh, maybe. A hundred years ago. Who knows? I wish I had
that whole hundred acres instead of just this here fifty. Got offered
two an acre for it. Two thousand. Enough to pay off the mortgage,
I guess."

He knew there had never been a dollar borrowed on the land
in all the time since the original grant. He looked at his cousin.

"Your American friend didn't like the army, eh?" Albert
scraped at his cheekbone with his right thumbnail.

"He never joined."

"A lot of them like that in Toronto now, I guess."

"Some."

"A little cowardly to my way of thinking."

"There's lots of ways to be cowardly." He looked out through
the dust on the window. "There's never been a mortgage on this
place, has there?" he said. "In more than your lifetime and mine
put together."

"Just a way of speaking," Albert said.

"You're quite a way from things here."

"Seven miles from the Rambler plant. Eight miles from the 401."

Modern loci. From the dusty front windows were still visible
the masonry walls of the river's mill, the ancient stone heart of the
locality. Tritavus.

"Lots of industry coming up," he said. "You might get General
Dynamics or Dow to build here."

"Can't tell. If you can't beat them hold out for top dollar on
what you got to sell them, I say."

"That's one way of looking at it, I guess."

"I guess."

WHEN THE DOCTOR came up from town he gave Shad a local anesthetic, and right there in the kitchen removed all the birdshot.

"Better keep your weight off it for two or three weeks," he said when he was done. "Then you'll be as good as ever."

"It's not going to work," Shad said on the drive back towards the city. "I could laugh last time, when they read off the Attorney-General's list and I said no, I never belonged to any of them, they're all dead, nobody belongs to any of them. And they said sure we know that and that's why we don't change them because when we did they just changed their names anyhow; now we keep the list the same and they don't change their names and we all know where we're at. They said all that and I laughed with them. But this time I'll throttle anybody who jokes about it or if they keep me waiting for five hours at a time. And if I go in, I'll kill somebody within three weeks. As soon as they start running me through their stamping machine. I'm not raw metal now; I'm a grown man. I've fought my wars. And if I stay out and hide out, some day my father'll die and I'll go back and they'll jail me for five years and I'll go mad and kill somebody. I dream of Bobby Washington some nights now, shooting that marine right off the stool, without giving him any warning at all, and I wake up in a worse sweat than after a game. I should have used the rifle myself."

He drove quickly and let Shad talk and fought the sense of failure that came as he considered that he had been unable to succeed even at the simple task of maiming a friend who desired physical maiming.

When they got on the high part of 401 the city was a sea of light right down to the harbour. Then darkness. Then the islands. Then the greater darkness beyond the islands.

ON THE RIVER

"WHAT IS IT? Really."

"There's nothing. It's nothing. Or you know what it is. The country's lovely. You'd better watch for the sign."

"Christ, you know I'm watching for the sign. But I need it like these crops need rain, not at all. Some of the most miserable moments of my youth were spent here. Summers. Even after ten years you don't forget roads."

"It's more like a trail."

"I'm going as slow as I can. You can't really expect gravel to stay long on top of straight granite."

"I'm sorry. I know you're taking it easy."

"It's the odds isn't it. The fifty-fifty."

"No."

THEY PARKED THE car by the barn. He knocked on the door of the house but nobody answered. He went out into the thin wedge of soil that made the vegetable garden and dug some worms. He felt the poverty of the land in the thinness of the mossy soil. The meadow was gone to weeds and he had to remember where the path had been. Age had worn it into the ground though, and once he could feel its pattern, he could not stray no matter how thick the weeds were. They were both damp almost to their knees by the time they reached the dock.

The boat was half-full of water and green with thin slime even after he had tipped all the water out by hauling the boat partially up on the dock. The near part of the bay was full of stumps and shore birds, but beyond that the river was clear and fresh looking.

"Let's just forget about it all, babe," he said. "Here I can promise you fish for sure."

Her face was beautiful and yet when he had turned from it for a minute its outlines and clarity blurred and he couldn't bring even a photograph of it back into his mind. It started to rain and she pulled a rain hat out of her pocket and adjusted it to cover as much of her hair as possible. Her gestures were still shy and cautious as though she were yet a girl. He pulled on the oars and took careful glances at her, measuring the angle of her cheekbones and the grace of her lips. Her eyes followed carefully the bobber as it danced on the water. If you took fine green glass, and filled it full of paraffin and a wick, and lit a flame that jogged and flickered as wind blew over the lip of the glass, that would be somewhat like her eyes. Her body was only beginning to bulge with this troublesome child and he realized that she was more appropriately dressed than he. The entire shore was totally familiar except where the brush had been cleared from what were hopefully cottage lots. It wasn't likely that people would come this far, he thought. Yet here was he with his city man's raincoat rowing in an almost water-logged boat. The oars dipped into the spools of fallen rain and he moved the boat farther from the shore.

They fished and let the boat drift. She used only a child's line with the worms he had dug from near the old farm house, and she caught, as he knew she would here at this time of year, whether it rained or not, innumerable small sunfish. She hooked a small bass from time to time and he carefully released those. He cast his own plugs farther and farther out, looking for something larger. They moved across the river and tried the deeper shore and then moved farther up to where a rocky point jutted out and where he remembered there would be bass and there were and she caught some more sunfish while he boated several bass—large enough to keep, if the season were open.

"You're getting cold," he said.

"No, I'm fine. I'm really fine."

"We're just compounding our illegalities, we'd better go in."

"If you insist."

He felt he should return the fish to their own cold depths, but he saw her face glisten with rain and a smile and he realized he wouldn't forget the way she looked there, so determined to keep herself under control despite everything and to enjoy their time on the water. It was a long row back to the dock, but the movement warmed him and the rain didn't get any worse and he was glad they hadn't drowned in the leaky, decrepit boat.

THEY CARRIED THEIR catch in the bailing bucket up the path to the barn. It had stopped raining and they began to feel the cold. He said that they ought to make a fire and she asked if she had not always been his furnace and pulled him towards her to kiss her, and their bodies, draped in clothes still wet from the river, met. He set down the bait bucket. They climbed into the loft which was full of dusty straw and they made love pleasantly and he could feel the fires within him and stronger within her and nothing was imperfect about it, except that he could not lose himself in his desire as he had once been able, he couldn't somehow get beyond the world and he felt that they were not as close as they had once been.

He told her he was going to clean the fish and bake them on

sticks against a fire and she said that was fine. He could tell that her anguish had caught her again and he did not mention what he had felt after the lovemaking nor ask her about that which she was choosing to hide from him. Her body was half hidden by the dusty straw and the lack of light from the rainy day. The first time she had been pregnant she had been awed by the changes in her body and had done a long series of sketches as her breasts slowly swelled and her hips widened and the child pushed her belly forward. She had made no sketches this time. He envied her ability to draw and kept his eyes upon the shapes of her body as long as he could without letting her know he was observing her.

HE STARTED A fire outside with dry straw from the barn and pieces of an old wagon seat which was rotting near the door. He cleaned the fish and set them on sticks in the ground so that they leaned near the fire and the fillets began to twist and curl about the sticks.

He didn't hear his uncle come up behind him.

"You the fellows that were out in my boat?"

"George. Hey, I thought you were the warden there for a minute. How've you been?"

"It's a dollar an hour for the boat and fifty cents for the worms. I seen you digging through the window."

He stood up and looked at the old man. His eyes were still clear, his skin was dark, yet faded from the bright red of old sunburning, haying days.

"There's better boats, but it's a dollar an hour."

He argued with this suddenly strange old man for four or five minutes, reminding him of family ties, asking after his wife Martha, even telling him the name of the horse that had once pulled the mowing machine that sat rusting in the barn. The old man blinked his eyes unnaturally, but did not seem to be listening at all.

"Martha left of cancer some time back," the old man said. "It's a dollar an hour for the boats."

"I'm your nephew, uncle George. For God's sake, I used to come here every summer for four or five years. I know you. You should know me. You must know me. I helped you caulk that very boat once. I've been to America; and I've come home. I remember you. I remember you used to laugh at old Jenkins down the road who'd only been here twenty years and got taken for his suspenders and his drawers when he bought a piece of land down near the locks. Once I came up in the winter and helped you fill the ice-house. I've looked up the family records. I know which regiment your grandfather was disbanded from when he settled here and how all the men felt cheated when they saw how much rock there was in the land and demanded larger allotments. Remember that? You may not know me, but I know who you used to be. I know where you came from. I know who you are now."

But the old man only looked at him somewhat queerly as if he couldn't understand why anyone would raise his voice at an old man. He realized that he had been shouting and he pulled out his wallet quickly and paid this old man three dollars for the time they had been out on the river and fifty cents for the worms. Because he didn't want his wife any more worried than she was now. The old man walked back up to the house and tried to lock the gate behind him, but it swung open and blew in the wind which was coming up after the storm.

She had come out to the door of the barn and was standing there with her eyes full of sorrow for him, that sorrow which he had always searched for when he was a young man and for which he had fallen so deeply in love with her, but he was sure of himself now, he didn't need that anymore, and he wanted suddenly to hurt her, or to make her at least present her weakest side in acknowledgement of submission.

"It's not the same," he said. "Nothing's the same." He glared at her for a moment but he couldn't sustain that confrontation. "Let's get the hell home. The fish is so charred nobody'll be able to tell what kind it is. I don't know why you keep bashing away at me. My whole life is flowing away looking after you."

She held herself stiffly and distant from him, as though she were willing the body which was softening for the child to a new hardness. The heater dried their clothes but she was careful to keep them neat about her as though she were a young virgin afraid of exposing herself.

WHEN THEY GOT back to the city there was no bread in the house so he went around the corner to the College Bakery to get some challah.

He took number 66, although he saw 65 had already been replaced, but there was a blond man in front of the cash register who seemed to be taking all of Mrs. Mier's time. He was obviously begging from her and she was shrugging her shoulders at him as though he were one of thousands she turned away every day. The two of them argued in a language he didn't try to listen to, and then Mrs. Mier took a loaf of bread from the counter and gave it to the blond man. Then she took ten dollars from the cash register and gave that to him also. The blond man walked out. He had been quite handsome obviously, but his face was flushed red with years of wine and his eyes looked as though they were looking away from the objects in the store, away from the ice cream freezer, the wedding cakes, the spiced meats, the displays of small delicacies.

"Ah," Mrs. Mier sighed. "What can I do for you?"

He ordered a loaf each of challah, rye, and whole wheat.

"You've been away," she said. "I don't see your wife so much anymore. To the country? All the English go up north for the summer. My husband he was always going to buy a little cottage, but the store took all the money and then he was gone."

"I'm not English."

"You're not Jewish?"

"I'm not Jewish."

"So what are you?"

"I'm an Indian," he said. She looked very unhappy and he wanted to joke with her and cheer her up.

"Sure, sure. You're dark, your wife's dark, and your little boy's got blond hair. Indians. You can never tell what's happening. You saw that man who was just in? John? He frightened your wife last time. His hair is not really blond. What can you do? He's from the same city in Europe as my husband, my own city. So we keep together here you know. And my husband always took care of him. At first we just gave him money; and when we had none we gave too. But then, you know, he was drinking; the world knew he was drinking. It was like pouring silver into a well. But my husband he never quit. He would just pay John's rent for him direct to the landlord, and take groceries over and try to get him jobs. But you just look at him now, he's not like ordinary. He would always quarrel, and fight even. Who fights? What's to do? My husband would be feeding and sheltering him, and he would take the welfare money or from the United and spend that on wine. Sweet wine. Ah, then he was sick. And now vodka. He would argue even with my husband. 'What's your reason?' my husband would shout at him. We knew that, we knew that. He saw the Germans kill his whole family. You can't deny him reasons for being like that. But we all did—see horror. It gets too much for me sometimes and I just go up to my bedroom and cry for four or five hours. I can't do anything except that and each time I feel that it won't work, that I'm going to fall apart from sorrow this time. But after four or five hours my children bring me a little something to eat and I go on. It's hard for them to understand and we drive them so and give them too much. They can't understand why we give them so much and take so little ourselves, but then sometimes later they do, they find out that we don't believe in all the things we collect about ourselves. And now it's worse for the ones up in the high part of the city. If the children understand that, sometimes they're all right; otherwise they go bad and we get drugs and disrespect for our troubles. Who can understand drugs? My son, he says John would be better off with marijuana. Can you believe that? But I think he's getting worse. I just give him money now. I don't know what to do. 'Mrs. Mier, you're rich,' he says, 'Look at all this about you; and three women in the back doing the baking. You're rich Mrs. Mier. I have nothing.' And ah, he frightened your wife. I can't understand that. She is so beautiful, and with the small boy. *Ich bin Yetzer Hara,* he said to her. I didn't want to give him any-thing, it seemed so useless, and then she came in and he said that to her and laughed at her. *Ich bin Yetzer Hara.* I thought that's why you were going to Dominion for your bread."

"My wife is pregnant," he said as he paid. "She's been having a bad time and the doctors say there's a good chance she'll lose the child."

"Ah, I didn't know. Why shouldn't she tell me? But if she's not sure. Ah, that John. Did he know? He is getting worse. It cannot be denied. How do you think he escaped? That is what he tor-ments himself with. How do you think I escaped? Because I gave them up? Some did that, you know. Just to save their own skins. Ah, he is worse. Here, take. Take for the child. All will be well. Ah, I'm sorry for John. Tell that to your wife. That a man from my own city should say such a thing."

She gave him an extra loaf of challah and he took it and left the clean store.

WHEN HE GOT home he put one of the loaves in the freezer compartment.

His son was kicking a many-coloured ball between the two brick walls which surrounded their garden. Though the boy was young, he could kick it hard enough so that it bounced from wall to wall and he could lose himself following it, turning and spinning and chasing after its flight. He wanted to go out and comfort his wife and have her drive out of him the fear that Mrs. Mier's story had brought, but the telephone rang. It was his broker and he stood there in the kitchen, staring through the windows at his wife and son, while this man who dealt in shares of other men's business and distant mines spoke to him about rising inflation and defending one's position. He listened to him, but he watched his own son, and he thought of his uncle George, and he remembered himself when he was not much older than his own son, skipping stones from the point where today he had caught the fish. Three of his friends had been caught in a sudden storm and drowned and he had developed a game where he skipped stones at death.

The waves were paperchases in furrows of blue questionings. The stones skipped between them.

Hello death, are you a porcupine?

Three skips.

Are you a Lancaster bomber carved of balsa?

Seven skips. Flat.

Are you the spring where deer come, half a mile beyond the CNR station, where the water has made the ground all mushy and you have to walk on a board path to get to the place where it fountains among the rocks?

One skip. Overconfidence. Beware.

Are you the men who hung Mussolini by his heels?

Four skips. Caught in a crest.

Do you like blueberries?

Three skips. First repeater. He is not a porcupine.

Hello death. Do you have trouble getting through the locks that join this lake to the next? Do you know what it means to portage? Is it you who turns the lightning to thunder? Does 7-Up like you? May I cross the river?

Ten skips. Second time. The answer to the tenth question is no. Come back again tomorrow. Try me tomorrow.

Goodbye child.

Goodbye death.

He went outside into the garden they had built in the midst of the city. There was only twenty-two feet between the wall of the funeral chapel and the wall of the coach house that had been turned from an artist's studio into two apartments, but they had filled the small space with grass and marigolds and odd pieces of stone work, angels and ornate stone flowers, which the mason who had built the house in the previous century had been unwilling to sell.

"The doctor phoned while you were out."

"Good news?"

"He said it was sixty-forty now."

"Well, that's better."

"I guess so."

"I shouldn't have been so sharp at the barn."

"I hope you're going to do something about your uncle."

"God, I don't know. I really don't know. He's my great-uncle really. There's nobody left of his generation, but that's not an excuse at all."

"I don't understand your family."

"They're solitary, that's true. The only thing that held them together was the queen I used to think, and of course that's absurd now. Now nothing holds them together. The land still frightens them. And poverty. I think everybody who came here was poor and is still afraid of it."

He lay down on the sheet in the late sun beside her, filled with an overwhelming love of her endurance.

"I don't understand you," she said, her anger breaking out. "I used to think I did, but I don't. Sometimes I think you want not to see me. Or to see me only as I used to be four or five years ago, when we were first together. When we used to spend all that time outdoors, running away from things. I get sick of it. I don't see why I should be afraid of saying it; I get sick of it."

He wanted to tell her that everything had been changed. That she was right. That he was sorry for how the blond man had frightened her. That he loved her for her courage of endurance, but he couldn't get those words to come out.

"I bought you some fresh challah—so your traditions don't die out in a new land. That was my broker on the phone. I'm even changing my opinions about them, the older ones. Somebody sent me some information about Levy Industries—which will double for sure—and I asked him about it. He told me I wouldn't want to get rich out of the war. Surprised the hell out of me. He said the money was really coming from war contracts, helicopter gears or something. You just can't escape it, I guess. Anyhow, I put the challah in the freezer. Mrs. Mier says hello and hopes you'll stop going to the Dominion."

"I'm not the same to you as I used to be. That's it, isn't it? That's what you said to me by the barn?"

"Look," he said, "you're right. I'm not arguing with you. Let's put the kid to bed and then we'll come back out here and lie on the sheet and watch the stars and ignore the bloody soot."

She agreed, her body loosening, and he realized that he had given in and by doing so had won a small victory. He knew he could never talk to her of the blond man, but he would be able to talk to her of how his gnawing desire for her had lessened as his fear of life had disappeared, as his acceptance of change and imperfection had increased almost miraculously, so that he no longer constantly desired to escape somewhere but was willing to accept everything, Mrs. Mier, the blond man from her city, his uncle George, the doctor's fluctuating odds, Levy Industries, everything, and still allow desire to overtake his body, and he realized somehow that what he had always desired had happened and that he had got, somehow, beyond certain desires which had blinded his early life.

In the evening, once the child was asleep, they would come out and lie on the sheet on the grass and be protected by the ugly brick walls which rose on all four sides of the small garden and he would be able to talk to her and reassure her. In the winter the new child would come, safely.

"Did the doctor say why the odds were better?"

"No. I don't know how he can tell without seeing me. He just said that if time goes by and nothing happens that even that is an improvement."

"Okay. Okay."

THE WAY WE DO IT HERE

IT WAS COLD again that third morning. Outside squalls and drizzle obscured the dawn. A day for bending the scope out of the way and relying upon your natural sight. Horace poured beer into the pancake batter and said it felt to him like a lucky day at last. Swede changed from one set of clothes patterned with dried blood to another only slightly less caked.

"Ah, feels good to get into something clean," Swede smiled. Smiling, he looked less than his thirty-five years, more like a college boy with the stack of girlie fold-outs under his hefty arm.

"Had a fellow up from Toronto once claimed he could quarter a moose without spilling a drop of blood on his white shirt. Said that three or four times. Wearing a white shirt. So I dropped a little four-hundred-pound moose calf in front of him one morning, a little grunter I hadn't even gutted. Just dumped two shots from the Lee Enfield into him, before 8 o'clock, and slung him into the boat fresh. 'Go to it,' I said. 'Get out the white shirt, Mr. Mulholland.' But he didn't feel up to it that particular morning, Mr. Mulholland didn't. You bet your hobnails he didn't. I like to step right inside a big grunter, with one boot each side of the ribs, and drive the butcher saw right through that hump. Now let's just put this little lady where the propane will shine on her countenance."

He moved Miss August over beside Miss September, onto the door of the food cupboard over the stove, so that light from the lamp-jet illuminated her glossiness, the jeweled derringer slung on her nude hip.

But nothing could irritate me, no sign of urban civilization. I had already accepted failure on this absurdly quick trip; I was looking forward only to a few more hours outdoors, even in the squall and drizzle, even if all I had to observe was the bravery of a wind-sniffing beaver, his nose and flat skull barely out of the rain-spattered water, tacking back and forth beyond the reddish Indian-tea bushes that made no attempt to hide my hunter's body. It's scent and noise you have to worry about with a moose; in the north their blindness is proverbial.

Traditionally, they will stand and let even a novice get five or six shots away at them, so long as he's got the wind in his face. And in this season, the heart of the fall, the males enter rut, trumpet across the miles, and come plunging conveniently to the lakeshore as soon as the hunter starts grunting. But we were short even the trumpeting. The day before I had tried to serenade a distant bugle — with no luck at all. Perhaps just as well. For we later decided that the bugle belonged to Swede, who had been working a different part of the lake with his two Milwaukee hunters. The others were disgruntled at the illusionary nature of this wooing, but it amused me almost as much as it did Swede.

"If I see that white plane spotting again, I'm going to have a pretty unsporting trophy," one of the men from Milwaukee said, somewhat bitterly. They had already been there five days.

One of them was a tavern owner and the other ran a small machine shop. The tavern owner had an immensity of gear, walkie-talkies and an emergency raft, and seldom spoke. The machinist deferred to the older man with whom he had been in the war and seldom was silent. He was proud of how he had built up his shop in a residential district by being very careful about his employees and when they arrived for work; he had only been caught after ten years, when a new machine was delivered by mistake at night when other men were at home. It was difficult to tell what their backgrounds were, but they both hated negroes and told stories of nasty rapes of nuns and young girls. They were very proud of the line that divided Milwaukee; they were ready to shoot the balls off any black bucks who crossed it intent on fulfilling the immense lusts they ascribed to them. They were both very good shots. One would skip a beer can far out over the lake and the other would shoot at it and try and keep it moving, spinning up into the air and bouncing off the water as it slowly crumpled and became shattered.

"Look at that, look at that," the machinist would say as the tavern owner shot. "That'll keep the bastards in their place."

"You should read some Fanon," I said.

"Is he dirty?"

"As only the French can be. All about Negro doctors treating white women."

"Is that right? We had quite a time over there during the war. I've got to get a shot at something. If that big Swede doesn't stop talking and put us within three hundred yards of something I'm going to dust the powder on that little white plane's nose."

My brother told of one such airplane hunter who had hopped out the door as soon as the plane landed, braced himself on the pontoon, and fired three shots dead into the engine, forgetting completely the inch or more of distance between the line of sight of his scope and the line of fire of his gun.

"You know," said Swede to me, "after I heard you grunting, I thought I may *have to* breed one of them cows, if we stay up here much longer. But I don't know if *you've* got enough meat on your bones to make it worth my while."

It was a good camp; we all joked and played stuke together and after a while the men from Milwaukee learned to stop talking about negroes.

Yet I wanted my brother to have some booty to return to town with. I felt I had deceived him somehow, by not making my intentions clear. He lives up there, well beyond the lakehead, in the same town with Horace and Swede. He would be there through the coming winter, long after I fled back to the slush of Toronto and my mod-tie students of Defoe, Thoreau, and Rilke.

"If I'm going to come up all that way," I had said when we were making the arrangements, "I want to go on a *real* hunt."

By which I had meant the exact opposite of what he assumed. For me, the truth of a hunt was tempered by visions and memories of a previous long hunt, just myself and one other lumberjack hunter, Jean Lorignal, pussyfooting for five hours through the bush near Chapleau before we saw anything, slugging out hundreds of pounds of meat by ourselves, and then the discord and bitterness that followed. Bitterness and discord of which I had not often thought.

There is still some real, walk-in hunting done around Fort Frances. Horace prefers it, but other methods are considered more stylish. And since I was coming seven or eight hundred miles, my brother had arranged for us to go the first-class way, the American plan. At Fort Frances we had loaded our gear and guns into one of Rusty Meyer's planes, a yellow Beaver, and flown some two hundred more miles deeper into the hinterland of Ontario.

Below, the land was an artist's mind, a photo-micrograph of unidentified cells. As with the Sahara, or the coastal forests of Africa, seen from above, there is so much pattern that the mind leaps to abstraction. The snake's movement of a river. Lakes adzed out of rock in imitation of a blackbird's erratic flights. Such

a massive fluxion that in the riot of shape and form it seems no artist would dare take a stance. We are too high to see a moose, even
the largest bull, but all four of us peer steadily down.

"Where are we headed," I asked, and saw the first omen of
failure arise. Horace pulled a map, roughly folded, out of a pocket
of his jacket, then spent five minutes before he could point out
our lake.

And when we settled down just before dusk, Swede was busily
adjusting a second motor on his boat so that he could cruise the
entire shoreline in one day.

The first day we did almost the same thing, cruised, but then
once Horace had fit the lake about him, we began moving up
creeks to inner lakes, found some fresh sign, watched a few runs
and some grassy shoreline. The second day we came around into
a bay of exactly the proper bogginess on shore. Near a beaver hut
there were bubbles in the murky water, and a lacework of fresh
track beyond the shore rank of trees.

So on the third morning, with the pick-up plane due to arrive
at noon, we felt some hope as we set out into the drizzle. The
wind had turned wrong for yesterday's bay, but that left it right for
several others we had spotted. It was too overcast for the small,
white American plane which had been bothering us, swooping
along the shoreline like an aluminium hawk, illegally spotting for
the hunters high and dry inside.

"A moose is dumb," Horace said. "It only seemed to take the
wolves a year or two before they'd avoid the sound of engines, but
the moose are learning. It may take them a generation or two, but
you can't tell me Mr. Whitewing's not keeping everything up in
the timber every time he flies around."

They dropped me off on a long point covering a good bay and
went ahead to scout a few others. The wind was hard. We had
put up a small bunch of teal and they had fled the bay with their

belly-down about twenty feet above the water. I settled the boat-cushion on the rocks and faced the rain. No more than five minutes after they had left me I heard a sound perhaps like shots or laughter, more like shouting, and I felt for my matches. If they had overturned I would have a cold day of it. I would have gone and looked, but the dawn was prime time and they were too good as boatmen to really permit worry.

And the wind came up the lake and across the bay like a hawk, a freshly stropped blade from Bunyan's razor. I hunched in further among the black spruce branches, let my mind descend into my body, and prepared to practise the cold austerities of the waiting hunt.

The beaver carried poplar back and forth bravely.

The teal returned.

With the wind, the yellow leaves caught and were caught by the damp sleet.

My gloves became drenched and my hands curved around one another for warmth.

I waited, running my eyes along the beaver swamp of the far shore, waiting for the slightest of movements in the shoreline trees, sighting in the three or four open shoreline spaces, re-estimating the distance across the water. Silent. Only hunter conscious.

One should be able, I know, to rest like that for the entire day. If you're on a good run, success is eventually inevitable. But success wasn't really why I was there. After two hours or so, my city-pampered body switched back on my mind. Look around, it said.

Behind me there was a grove of my favourite conifers, shaggy, old black spruces; reaching up almost sixty feet. Not bad for them, this far north. I slid in among their quietness to knead some life back into my hands, to stretch up my back. To feel again beneath my feet that natural deep pile of moss, needles, and brush you find only in rich, old forests: reindeer-moss, black crowberry, spoonleaf sphagnum, ground cedar, bracken fern, dwarf juniper, running clubmoss. I had no need of identifying them, only of running some of the possible names through my mind, of feeling that inimitable crunch as each particular welcome mat gave beneath my feet. If that moment's fear were true, if the boat that brought me had in reality overturned, I could take some reindeer-moss and dry it for flour. A world of chill possibilities was around me. And of memory.

ON THE MOOSE hunt I had been trying not to remember, we had just pussyfooted up on a whole family of moose, through far thicker brush than this, earlier in the year when all the leaves were still on, through a half mile or so of nearly pure hazel bush and little balsam trees.

They were down in a pothole, a little bowler hat upside down, shaped just as though it had been scooped out for a washbasin. We could have walked right by them, but they must have decided to come up just as we were passing around the rim.

"Psst, psst," said Lorignal. "Behind you, my friend." And he would have laughed if he hadn't been so determined on that trip. He was about ten yards in front of me. He said that all he could see were two brown patches, but I was near enough to make out the outline of the bull's hump. I did a more dangerous thing than by then I had ever even considered.

I fell to the matted, tangled rug of the forest to let Lorignal shoot over me. I remember thinking, in small consolation before I dropped: at least neither of them is facing me. Although I knew too how quickly one slug could change their mind about which way to run, and to trample.

We were lucky; we had to be lucky on that trip. Lorignal and I. With one gun between the two of us.

He was a city refugee too, club-footed, who had left Montreal three years previously because there his strength and his flaw both seemed to work against him. Despite his twisted foot, he was strong. In the north he had turned himself into one of the richest lumberjacks of the region, the sound parts of his body hardened and strengthened, the right leg became tough as a kangaroo tail. So that he could easily outrun me in his leap-and-hop fashion: the strong foot down, thrust and movement; the crippled foot barely contacting the earth as he hopped on it, almost as though it were not a part of his body, a vaulter's pole that at any moment he might release, at the apogee of his leap; then thrust and movement again.

Moi, the university had just finished dumping a year's supply of ideals into my mind while crimping my spirit with its innate snobbery, its unresolved class tensions and distortions; so that I for learned reasons and Lorignal for experienced ones had together jumped to the support of a M. Blaise, the union man for that region, in his fight to organize Kapela's mill and camp, in his struggle to get the minimum wages heading up closer towards the dollar an hour mark. A bitter fight. Kapela did not have a big operation. One man had made it, and was still there, and was determined to see what he had created grow and prosper.

The best workers left at the first sign of trouble; a lot of those who remained were old or flawed, refugees from Hungary or the Gaspe. There was violence. Bitterness. Scabbing. Sand-bagging. We won, eventually. The idealists and the refugees. M. Blaise signed an agreement with Kapela and spent an evening drinking vodka with him. The company store became a co-operative. The mill cut its work week to only fifty hours. And Kapela took the offered chance to fire seven or eight of the least productive workers and thus to make his woodcrews more efficient.

It was for the let-go workers that Lorignal had gone hunting.

Without a gun, I was just a companion and meat-carrier, but I felt some of his guilt. Blaise had been the organizer of the struggle, but Lorignal its hero and I its brain.

So he took the chance and shot across me, clean into the bull's hump so that it did drop at once and turned not upon us, the source of its pain. The cow turned equally quickly from her vanquished companion and in the turning was gone, with her calf, lost among the thick hazel and balsam.

"Cow's tender, but I like meat with a little character," said Lorignal. And we set to the hard work.

It took us two trips, in and out, more than six miles each way. Lorignal wanted it all there for the presentation he had planned. We slept one night in the woods and it was nearly noon the next day before we had the meat all packed out.

The fired men and their families were all packed up, into two old Studebakers and a red Ford pick-up. Bedsprings jounce-jangled on the car roofs.

They refused the meat. Out of pride, or a sense of betrayal, or just because they were unsure of their destination and whether they had room for it, or because it was not quite legally the moose season and they suspected a trap. I never worked it out.

But they refused it. Bitterly. Telling Lorignal he would need it himself for all the work he would be doing that winter. Suggesting what he could do with one of the moose legs. "Jouk aside, Frenchy, or I'll shove that leg bone a mile up your garbage hole," one said. Standing beside the two old Studebakers that hadn't run all summer. There are few bitternesses equal to that of a poor man let go for inadequacy.

And Lorignal understood them. Scruffy little men he could have booted into the sawdust pile — even with his twisted foot. He didn't press it on them. He just bantered back at them and told them how he would enjoy the heart for lunch.

AND JEAN DID that. We split the heart and said nothing about their refusal. But Jean Lorignal avoided tradition, he carried the quarters back into the bush and left them there for the lynx cats; he did not divide the flesh among the successful. He gave none to Blaise; none to Kapela; nothing but the heart to himself.

MY HANDS WERE warm in the black spruce grove. I had been knuckling them and blowing on them all the time the story walked through my mind. "Let's go pussyfooting here," I told myself. And I moved slowly among the drooping trees, and out of them. Towards the beaver swamp and its fallen aspen poplar and tacamahac. Looking in the bog of mud and broadleaves for track. Grunting expectantly, although I really expected nothing.

And it was there my brother and Horace found me. Coming up by the beaver hut, past fallen trees which reached towards their boat.

"It's not that shallow," I said. "Watch the deadfalls and come up."

"We're full of moose, you know," they said.

"You're what?" I am back in a dream.

"We got one."

But I hadn't known. The wind disguising the shots. The shouting not for disaster, but one shot from each of their guns. And perhaps a bit of laughter.

While I had been sitting and pussyfooting, they had been quartering. There is an essential ugliness to a moose, especially when his body is broken into four. This one filled the bottom of the boat, his rib-cage exposed to the drizzle, one bare knee-knuckle jostling the wind, the sleet laced and globed in small mazes on the bristly fur.

"Pretty ugly booty," I said.

"A pretty ugly country," Horace smiled.

But just sitting in the boat, it warmed us on the return trip down the lake. And warmed me as I saw one of the ugly haunches, clad in a voyage-stretched, old, blue, duffel bag, slide out of Air Canada's mechanical luggage sorter at the Toronto International Airport, and hang there for a reluctant moment, prevented by its weight and inertia from sliding down the revolving steel cone amidst the shiny luggage of other passengers. And the ugliness warmed me as I thought of Horace, secretively nodding to me as he slung the unskinned portions up into the Beaver: "He's not saying much, your brother; but he really enjoyed that. He really enjoyed it all. You'll have to come up here more often."

THE HARD-HEADED COLLECTOR

THEY CAME THROUGH the mountains themselves unscathed, although Piet Catogas nearly tumbled into the gorges beneath Yellowhead Pass when his horse skittered out from under him. The last horse. When they entered North Battleford they were all seven afoot, but they were well entertained in front of the tent of the bread baker, who kept them amused with juggling tricks and poured them many cups of hot tea in blue galvanized cups filled to the brim then with swirling milk.

The bread baker's final trick was to keep seven round oranges up in the air at once, and when the rotund man had heard enough of their clapping he gave one orange to each man. His own children clustered around and his wife walked back into the tent, so the men were careful to divide, but Pier Dela Ombre, throwing his filthy black hair out of his eyes so that the firelight could blaze back out of his pupils, asked for a second orange from Piet Catogas, the leader, and began to explain to the children why the earth did not fall into the sun. He sang to them.

Katrina, the wife of the bread maker, came out of the tent and said to her husband, "Why not offer Mr. Dela Ombre two loaves of wheat bread every morning so that he will be encouraged to stay here?"

The bread maker stated the offer to Piet, but Piet refused. "We are on our way to a strange land and there is not one man that I can afford to lose. We have the return journey on our minds too."

Pier Dela Ombre's orange sun rotated around and around the orange earth held stationary by little Katrina, the bread baker's only daughter. The mother smiled.

At midnight, when all the men except Ole Siuk and Scrop Calla were seated around the fire drinking the white lightning which the Scottish whisky maker distilled in North Battleford, Katrina came out of the tent with the bread baker.

"We will give you your own tent," she said directly to Pier Dela Ombre. "And a complete set of the *European Encyclopedia,* and after twenty years' service a golden shovel. Which will no doubt help to make you feel glorious as you clear away the blizzards from your door or clean out the many ashes from your stove. Around here we have very little anthracite."

Pier Dela Ombre smiled and said that he needed no time to consider their kindness. "We do not even know how far we now need to travel," he said to the woman, "but we must be there by May and then there is the long journey back before we can really set down to work, and for each stage I will have to learn the new strophe that the good Calla writes. In fact, if he were not out now stealing the settlement's horses, he would probably be putting one together, telling of our dangerous passage through the mountains. I cannot stay."

They both laughed at his humour of the horses and determined even more to persuade him to stay.

"Little Katrina will be disappointed you were unable to explain to her the proportions of the sun and the earth," the woman said. "At times in the summer I have heard her say that they almost seem equal. It does get very hot here in the summer, but we arrange many boat picnics on the Saskatchewan, and of course there is nothing like sawdust to keep the winter's ice safely stored."

They kept after him, gently, until the bread maker fell asleep.

Ole and Scrop came back very early in the morning, before the sun, but little Katrina had risen and was adding yeast to the sugar water for the day's baking.

"If you let him stay long enough to explain the proportions of the earth and the sun," she said to Piet, "I will not awaken my father and tell him that the man with the sunken eyes has taken possession of Elder Clough's grey horse and silver bridle. And six other poorer horses."

Piet nodded to Pier Dela Ombre. He laid the golden orange of the sun on the ashes of last night's fire and took Katrina by the hand.

"If the sun were made that small," Pier said, "let us say about a thousand to one, then the earth would still be so large that in a whole day we could not walk around its edge."

He held her hand more tightly and began walking with her away from the tent and the fire, in the gentle circle of one who is uncaringly lost.

The six men were glad to have the extra horse and the mountains behind them, with the summer not completely gone.

"He'll be in real trouble when they discover the loss," Scrop Calla said to Piet when they next stopped.

"The mother will get him out of it," Piet replied. "If the little girl can't. God, they start them young here. I can't believe there's anywhere they start them so young. Even among the Sasarians."

Why had he decided to present the works to the United States?

"Well, a lot of people wanted it . . . but I couldn't do what I did in any other country. What I did I accomplished here in the United States. It belongs here."

Did he have any comment about President Johnson? "I told him I've adopted him. I love him."

They went eastward safely for five days across the lush prairie grass until they heard gunfire in the distance ahead and what they thought might be a tornado, a dust storm. Coming over the rise they saw a Nanarian Indian from one of the reserves who shouted at them as he drove his almost collapsing wagon at a dangerous pace towards the west. His wife and children sat on mounds of hay in the back, firing whence they had come. The men rode on, although they knew there was a fire ahead which would block their way.

"We can return later," Piet said, "and cross over the ashes. Or look for the river again."

"I'm sure I can find it if you let me lead," said Torah Black.

He rode back whence they had come—the mountains were invisible—and the others followed, although Piet had said nothing.

The wagon was overturned less than a mile to the west. Besides the wife and the four children there was a milkwhite goat among the hay. "This will save us all," Black said and slit its throat. He held it by the hind legs as it kicked its way to death and circumscribed a large circle around the wagon, the men, the four children, and the woman.

"We had better ride on," Piet said.

After a time the firing started again, and once or twice the five men could distinguish the sound of Torah Black's shotgun. Scrop Calla could see the gold engraving on its stock glittering in the sun.

"What does a gunsmith know about old superstitions," Piet said as they rode back eastward over the powdery black ashes. Looky McLaww nodded sagely.

Mr. Hirshhorn lives with his fourth wife, Olga, in Greenwich. He is the father of six children, two of them adopted, and is a grandfather several times over. He is board chairman of the Callahan Mining Company, and the principal stockholder in Prairie Oil Royalties, a Canadian concern.

He has been trying to follow doctor's orders to take it easy, but finds it a trial. When he appears at Parke-Bemet, the auctioneer knows that he has to keep a sharp eye for the little man with the expressive face who signals vigorously with his program. If there is any doubt, Mr. Hirshhorn lets the auctioneer know what he is up to. He calls out his bids in a loud clear voice.

"He's a tiger," an old, close friend said.

Beyond the death of Torah Black they had no more difficulties until they reached Winnipeg. It was difficult to find a place that would take all of them, for the Leagues were busy, but eventually they found a large old house on the river in Ste. Vital. All of the girls spoke French so that Andre was kept busy as a translator; but after all, what is there to say?

"We have made it over the hard part," Piet said. "We have still eight months to go. Let us hope that the winter will be easy. Tonight you may enjoy yourselves; there is no more need of the horses in any case."

The first girl did not satisfy Looky because the pleasure of her body simply filled his head with memories of the wife he had left on Queen Charlotte Island.

"That damn Hunky won't want more than a snack," he said and walked into Ole Siuk's room and threw him out of bed. "J'ai une qualité inestimable," he said to the girl and she shone with delight.

"He is afraid for his wife," Piet said to Ole Siuk. "There are many other carvers and poets on the island. She is a loving model; puts her heart into it."

"Mineur, how's about a free and equal exchange of riches," Looky later said to Andre. But when Andre tried his new girl he found her cold and exhausted. She swung a condom full of black beetles over his head and threatened him with death.

Looky took Scrop Calla's girl also, a plumper one than the first three, but when he came to Piet's room he found him gone.

The old woman, the girl provider, still lay in the bed and offered herself to Looky, but she was dark-haired and hidden-eyed like Looky's wife and he could not take her.

"There's the matter of the bill," she said, "but that's not important. I have the horses. If you had slept with me those bay-tàrds would have beaten you to death with horseshoes on the end of pikes and we would have put you out in the stable to freeze until spring, but as it is you will save us the cost of putting an ad in the *Free Press* for some able body to haul our ashes all winter."

"At least McLaww won't have to go about with a gold shovel in his hands," Piet Catogas said to Scrop Calla as the four men trudged on bear-paw snowshoes through the wine-dark snows north of Fort Frances, as the sun fell.

But, with the end of World War I, he guessed wrong on the market and found his fortune had shrunk to $4,000. Mr. Hirshhorn says he has always learned by his mistakes. At any rate, he was back on top in a few years and intuitively got out of the market with $4 million just before it broke in 1929.

When he was a child, Mr. Hirshhorn was attracted to the pictures on the Prudential Life Insurance Company's calendars.

Mr. Hirshhorn was attracted to the possibilities of Canada, bought 470 square miles of land and, by 1950, was mining uranium. His biggest coup occurred in 1952. On the advice of Franc Joubin, a geologist who had little audience elsewhere, Mr. Hirshhorn secretly put together 56,000 square miles of claims in Ontario's Algoma Basin and struck a uranium bonanza in Blind River.

When the four men were only twelve miles from Chapleau, they came across a group of Hémonites at prayers. These had built a great square wall of snowblocks out onto the lake, no more than a foot high, and at intervals, dressed in brown worsted cowls, stood women, men, and the older children, praying into the sky.

"This is a chance for Calla to use his four iamb line," said Ole Siuk, who had taken over the post of religious cynic since they had lost McLaww.

Piet could see no altar, but in the centre of the square was a tall ancient man standing above a slender circular hole cut deep into the ice down to the dark water below.

"In the summer you can see clear down thirty-two feet," the old man said.

Near him were three boys tending nine blanketed cattle. On a high easel, facing in the direction in which all prayed, was an old lithograph of an Essex County dairy farm, coated in plastic to protect it against the weather but torn in one corner so that the gold of cut hay was stuck to a piece of flapping plastic and glittered in the frosted sunlight.

"No one will do it," the old man said.

"I'm out of grass, acid, and mushrooms," said Scrop Calla, "but I know what you want and I will attempt it."

He stripped himself naked and lowered himself into the water three times so that not only his heavy beard and hair were covered with a silver of ice, but his whole body. It shone.

He held his arms outward in the direction of them all and said loudly and with no sound of rhythm: "I know, I know, I know."

Upon the horizon appeared, as though on the edge of a highly polished silver punch bowl, a simple inverted image of all: the penitents, the wall of snowblocks, the old priest, Scrop Calla, the strangers, and the forests and the snow-covered meadows behind them. With the exception that, in the inverted image, the cows were unblanketed and moved about freely: their udders thick with milk, their coats sleek as threshed grain.

"You're a genius and a half," the old priest said. "You'll have to settle here. In the summer you can see down thirty-two feet and the fishing licence's only two bucks—to natives that is."

"During the war," said Piet to Ole Siuk as they came near French River, "Calla once deserted and tried to find the enemy, but a handful of men went unknowingly after him and became so enthused with their fear that they broke through the lines of the Sasarians and covered themselves with loot and glory."

At night when they stopped now, Ole Siuk read in Calla's leather-bound notebooks and occasionally was seen stamping his left foot heavily and repeatedly on the hard earth of the world.

"Poverty has a bitter taste," Mr. Hirshhorn said years later, recalling how his mother was sent to the hospital when a fire gutted their tenement on Humbolt Street, and the family was dispersed to various homes in the neighborhood. "I ate garbage."

In French River the three men were fed and lodged in a building as tall as the smallest of the foothills they had long left behind them.

"Perhaps we have gone far enough," said Andre. "That is a building tall enough to house Egsdrull. The tools must be rusty and I long to hear the chips shatter, even a practice stroke."

All of the people there had a small exact circle of soot on each cheek, but they were kind to the voyagers, gave them fat for their stiff-thonged snowshoes, and did not laugh loudly at Ole Siuk's awkward attempts at song.

"You can see God's fish," they said at the end of the recital. "Perhaps then you will stay and teach us to sing."

Inside the tall building sat rows and rows of old men and women, all dressed in heavy blue robes, but seemingly divided into three groups.

Some had two circles of dark soot on their cheeks, so that only the blue robes distinguished them from the guide. These sat reading from a book that was passed slowly down the rows, meditating while they awaited their turn. Others had only one circle of soot, that on their right cheek, and were busy at work benches, hammering tiny marbles of gold into large, almost circular flakes. Their blue robes seemed cumbersome, and many seemed too old for such a task.

The third group had no marks on their cheeks, but on their foreheads was a slightly larger, more oval, circle of soot. These seemed to be neither reading nor hammering, but once, while the strangers were there, one of the old men among them went up to the forty-foot fish which dominated the entire building, a *mashki-noje*. Only its skeletal frame was finished; the outer covering was not yet half done. The old man laid in place on the others his own interlocking golden scale. Then fire consumed him.

"Each year," said the guide, "we get just about done before the Sasarians come raiding. We've calmed the Nanarians. One year the Sasarians will be awed by God's fish and will allow us to finish. Below God's fish, you will see the coffins of the fifty original scale craftsmen. Each holds an ivory tooth on his breast, and on the day that the Sasarians are awed, they will all arise and the teeth will complete the fish of unity."

When Piet and Ole left, Andre Mineur was talking in Arabic to the God's fish's tail. He was not speaking of their own voyages and their many losses.

"He's a sucker, that Mineur," said Piet Catogas to Ole Siuk as they crossed the St. Lawrence at Three Rivers. "It won't sell. I've seen men making them in Boston, twice the size, every scale machine-polished, and for half the price."

"I think you have the right reason," said Ole Siuk. "Hah, hah, hah." His teeth had all fallen out because of the bad diet they had endured during the winter and he looked very old and ugly.

"It's almost the end of April," he said.

The President added:

"*Washington is a city of powerful institutions — the seat of govern-ment for the strongest government on earth, the place where democratic ideals are translated into reality. It must also be a place of beauty and learning, and museums should reflect a people whose commitment is to the best that is within them to dream. We have the elements of a great capital of beauty and learning, no less impressive than its power.*"

The two men avoided all contact with the Sasarians, although Piet was certain he could communicate with them if necessary, but when they arrived in Edmundston and stated that they were determined to reach the Bay of Chaleur even though only two of them remained, they ran into the united opposition of all the Town Fathers.

"The *day* of judgment is only possible as a concept because of our notions of the duration of time," the Mayor said. "In reality there is a summary court in perpetual session and we're going to beat your knackers down to your knees."

They turned upon Siuk, stripped off all his clothing, tore away his finger nails with their teeth, gnawed his fingers with the fury of famished dogs, and thrust a sword through one of his hands. They drove the two men between them in a hastily formed aisle, and beat them with clubs and thorny sticks. Then they hung them by the wrists to two of the poles that supported the Town Hall. A woman was commanded to cut off Piet's thumb, which she did; and a thumb of Siuk was also severed, a clamshell being used as an instrument, in order to increase the pain.

In the morning the children came to castrate them, and then they were set free. Hair was pulled from their beards and their wounds were lacerated before they left.

In the night Ole Siuk wrote out a message for Piet, the leader, although he did not awaken him.

"I guess I've followed Areskoui and that crew long enough. I feel the need of those Edmundston men more than anything.

My great-aunt was a nun in the Ukraine, but she was of unsound motives in her religious pursuits. When she was not made Mother Superior at a time she had appointed, she stripped herself naked during a Sunday mass and declared herself to the world as an atheist. The family has had bad luck ever since. Maybe this act of mine will atone in some way. I wouldn't visit us, however, on your way back. I'll probably be married to the woman who collects thumbs."

Piet had no one to talk to, but he chuckled to himself as he came upon the birch bright sea.

"It's lucky old McLaww didn't make it to that part of the contest. He would have hated me for the rest of his life."

"This is a magnificent day for the nation's capital and for millions of Americans who will visit Washington in the years to come," the President said, smiling at Mr. Hirshhorn at his side.

"Throughout the world," the President said, *"Mr. Hirshhorn has sought the great art of our time—those expressions of man's will to make sense of his experience on earth, to find order and meaning in the physical world about him, to render what is familiar in a new way."*

It was late June when he arrived at the bay.

"I've come for Egsdrull," said Piet to the manager of the lumber yard. "I'm the carver from Queen Charlotte." He handed him the receipt.

"You're a *little* late," replied the manager. "And as well there's the little matter of the seven terms: shape an axe, sing its joints, engrave its shaft, bless its point, name it in ten tongues, knit soul and intent, determine where lies its enemy."

"I had men who could do all that. Ole Siuk could have shaped it out of brittle rock; Pier Dela Ombre was once with the Scalla; the best man with a graver you ever saw was Torah Black; Looky McLaww would have had a libation for the blade; Andre Mineur knew a baker's-dozen tongues; Scrop Calla would have taught

you a thing or two about serpents biting their own tails and how
to hoop a barrel hoop. And I, why do you think I came all this
way? Put that axe in my hands and show me the tree, show me
Egsdrull, and God himself will not be able to catch the bloody
chips."

"Terms is terms," the manager said. "The sea probably has
fish who could do all that, but you don't see him standing there
begging."

Piet could find nothing to say.

"I've got something out behind the slab pile that might do for
you," the manager said. "We flooded those ten or twelve years
back when we gave up hope on you."

Beyond the slab pile, where a small red fork-lift truck scurried
with its swaying load of sixteen- and eighteen-foot slabs, was a
scene of desolation. The creek which once had there flowed into
the Bay of Chaleur was dammed. Forty feet or more on either
side was flooded. All the trees that once had grown there were
black stubs. Not ankle high, as a good piece of future meadowland
might look waiting for the years to rot the stumps, but man high,
totem high: trunks like amputated limbs.

"You're free to make something of one of those if you like,"
said the manager. "But I don't expect any of them is fit for a trip
back to the coast. Hollow rotten."

"I did not come all that way," said Piet. He was screaming.
"Lose all those men, suffer all that laceration. Father, father, I am
a grown man. You promised me Egsdrull. I discovered the Pacific;
I fed China for three months; I played poker with Lord Astor; I
kissed the dirty Hun's lady. I courted death. You have forsworn
me. Thiefman."

"Forsworn you, my ass. Terms is terms. There it is in black and
white. Ninth of May or all terms void. Seven terms to be fulfilled
before delivery. It's time you earned your daily bread for a change,

young fellow. Don't father me. Perhaps we can fit you in on the butt-saw, if you can keep up. You're not so spry as you once were. What do you say, young fellow? Want to try Newfoundland?"

President Johnson formally accepted the Hirshhorn art collection today "on behalf of the American people" in a ceremony at noon in the Rose Garden of the White House.

Piet Catogas lasted a week at work before his death. Not on the butt-saw, which is a skilled task and requires a young and agile man, but out in the yard in the sunlight, sorting the lumber by lengths, widths, and grades.

This was a job for the young or the very old, but he found no sympathy among his comrades and was unable to speak to them of the carvings that he had made before he was half their age, back on the island.

More than one of his wounds was infected, and though he bathed in the warm sea he knew it was futile and awaited his death with great equanimity. At night he wondered if Dela Ombre would have blond sons later with Katrina or what Torah had thought about as he fired into the flame and smoke; he chuckled at the thought of Looky beaten by the horseshoes on pikes and wondered how many winters Calla would survive; he was afraid Mineur had sold out to those madmen and prayed for Ole Siuk.

In the mornings he slept later and later. He would have been fired on the morning he died if ever he had reached the yard where men sorted the sixteen-foot one-by-sixes into four grades without a passing glance at the ship which came for his body.

ACKNOWLEDGEMENTS

"The Generation of Hunters," "An Opening Day," "Flying Fish," "Fulfilling Our Foray," and "Mud Lake: If Any" in slightly different form, appeared originally in *Saturday Night*.

"The Way We Do It Here" was first printed, somewhat shortened in *Ontario 67*.

"The Hard-Headed Collector" appeared in *The Tamarack Review* initially.

Particular thanks must be directed to Kildare Dobbs, for it was he who admitted the bias in the average Canadian reader against stories of this breed of reality and yet not only invented the disguise under which many of them found their way into print but encouraged the creation and publication of the full work. The Canada Council kindly provided a short-term grant during the summer of 1967 when much of the final rewriting was completed. An unknown *New York Times* humourist unwittingly provided some of the phrases in the final story.

DAVE GODFREY was born in Winnipeg, Manitoba, in 1938. A writer, publisher, and academic, Godfrey published three works of fiction: the novel *The New Ancestors*, winner of the Governor General's Literary Award for Fiction, and the short story collections *Death Goes Better with Coca-Cola* and *Dark Must Yield*. He was co-founder of both House of Anansi and New Press, and ran Press Porcépic with his wife, writer Ellen Godfrey. He studied at the University of Toronto, Iowa, and Stanford, and taught literature at the University of Toronto and the University of Victoria. Dave Godfrey died in Victoria, B.C., in 2015.

LIST

The A List

Basic Black with Pearls Helen Weinzweig

Ticknor Sheila Heti

This All Happened Michael Winter

Kamouraska Anne Hebert

The Circle Game Margaret Atwood

De Niro's Game Rawi Hage

Eleven Canadian Novelists Interviewed by Graeme Gibson

Like This Leo McKay Jr.

The Honeyman Festival Marian Engel

La Guerre Trilogy Roch Carrier

Selected Poems Alden Nowlan

No Pain Like This Body Harold Sonny Ladoo

Poems for all the Annettes Al Purdy

Five Legs Graeme Gibson

Selected Short Fiction of Lisa Moore

Survival Margaret Atwood

Queen Rat Lynn Crosbie

Ana Historic Daphne Mariatt

Civil Elegies Dennis Lee

The Outlander Gil Adamson

The Hockey Sweater and Other Stories Roch Carrier